DOCTOR WHO
AND TH... ...STAR

G000272972

DOCTOR WHO
AND THE
HAND OF FEAR

Based on the BBC television serial *The Hand of Fear*
by Bob Baker and Dave Martin by arrangement with
the British Broadcasting Corporation

TERRANCE DICKS

A TARGET BOOK
published by
the Paperback Division of
W. H. ALLEN & CO. LTD

A Target Book
Published in 1979
by the Paperback Division of W. H. Allen & Co. Ltd
A Howard & Wyndham Company
44 Hill Street, London W1X 8LB

Printed in Great Britain by
Richard Clay (The Chaucer Press) Ltd
Bungay, Suffolk

ISBN 0 426 20033 0

Contents

Prologue

The planet was dying.

On the surface of Kastria, nothing moved, nothing lived. Lashed by constant snowstorms, scoured by solar winds, Kastria was bleak, deserted, dead.

It was very cold in the observation dome. A sinister-looking figure wrapped in his thick, hooded cloak, Zazzka sat shivering at the control console, studying the monitor screen. A tiny blip of light moved across it with infinite slowness as the capsule it represented hurtled through deep space.

A voice crackled from the console speaker. 'Central Command to Zone Six. Central Command to Zone Six. Report immediately.'

'Obliteration module on course, and at normal function. Dome temperature continues to fall.'

'You are not Technician Oban.'

Zazzka glanced at a huddled shape in the corner. 'Technician Oban no longer functional. He has died from the cold. This is Commander Zazzka.'

'Computer time for capsule detonation?'

'The capsule has been projected through the space warp. It will reach a distant solar system in six time units. Power-levels are falling rapidly. Contact may soon be lost.'

'Report on barrier condition.'

'Deteriorating steadily.'

There was a pause. The voice said, 'The North has already fallen. When the South Barrier collapses temperature loss will intensify rapidly.'

'Surface operation will no longer be possible,' said Zazzka flatly. His strangely constituted body had immense resilience, but he knew that if he remained on the surface of the planet for much longer he would die like all the others.

There was another pause, then the voice spoke again. 'Confirmed. Here are new orders. Switch capsule control through to me, here at Central Command. I shall detonate the module *now*, before contact is lost.'

'But King Rokon, total obliteration of Eldrad was ordered. Computer indicates premature detonation would give a one in three million chance of particle survival——'

'*We have no choice!* Switch control to me now, then evacuate the observation dome.'

'I obey, your majesty.' Zazzka's hands moved stiffly over the controls.

High above a primitive planet, the Kastrian obliteration capsule sped through space like some wandering meteor. Inside, its occupant lay stretched out like a corpse in a coffin. But he wasn't dead, not yet. He lay clamped in unbreakable bonds, listening to the voice in his ear. The prisoner knew that when the voice ended, his life would end with it. He lay motionless, listening. Only his right hand with its great jewelled ring clenched and unclenched convulsively.

8

The voice was that of King Rokon, the one who had condemned him to this fate. It was old, and full of malicious satisfaction.

'Eldrad, slayer of the Vox Libra,' said the voice in a kind of chant.

'Eldrad, transgressor of the order,
Eldrad, carrier of all evil,
Eldrad, destroyer of the barriers,
Eldrad, saboteur, genocide, anarch ...'

(Far away on Kastria, the wizened hand reached for the control that would trigger the capsule's self-destruct mechanism.)

'Eldrad, sentenced to obliteration ...'

(The finger stabbed down ...)

In the few seconds of life that remained to him, one thought filled the prisoner's mind. 'No! Eldrad must live! *Eldrad must live!*'

As the capsule disappeared in a soundless explosion, his massive body shattered into a thousand fragments. Yet, due to some freak of the blast, one part of him still survived ... The right hand was flung free of the explosion. Down, down it spun until at last it buried itself deep into the primeval mud of the planet below.

There it stayed, for one hundred and fifty million years ...

1

The Fossil

The bare, rocky area was completely deserted—and for a very good reason.

With a wheezing groaning sound a battered old blue police box appeared from nowhere. The door opened and a very tall man stepped out. He wore loose, comfortable clothes with a tweedy Bohemian look about them. The outfit was topped off with an immensely long scarf and a broad-brimmed soft hat jammed on to a tangle of curly hair. He stared about him with wide, curious eyes. The police box had landed in a rocky valley just beneath a cliff. The ground was littered with rubble, and the wind snatched up clouds of dust and swirled them through the air.

A little apprehensively, the man glanced over his shoulder.

'It's a bit windy, I'm afraid, Sarah.'

An attractive dark-haired girl came out of the police box, adjusting the scarf in her hair. She looked disgustedly around her. 'Earth, he says! Earth for certain, this time. Hah!' She folded her arms and glared fiercely at the tall man, who was that mysterious traveller through Space and Time known as the Doctor. Sarah Jane Smith had been his companion on a variety of terrifying adventures. Now she had decided that enough was enough, and asked to be taken home.

The Doctor was doing his best, but unfortunately the steering mechanism of the TARDIS was somewhat erratic, and previous arrivals had been in the wrong place, and the wrong time. From the look of things it had happened yet again. Sarah was beginning to feel that the planet Earth in the last quarter of the twentieth century was the one place and time she was never going to see again ...

The Doctor by contrast was utterly confident—but then, he always was. 'Don't worry, Sarah, this is Earth all right.'

'This? This howling wilderness is Earth?'

'That's right.'

'Unlike you, I happen to be a native of Earth—South Croydon to be precise—which is where you said we'd arrive.' Sarah looked at the rocky desolation around them. 'I can tell you categorically, Doctor, this is not South Croydon.'

'Would you settle for the South Coast?' asked the Doctor hopefully.

'South Coast! This isn't even Earth, I tell you.'

'Bet you a stick of rock!'

'Well, if it is Earth, it's the middle of the Gobi desert.'

'It does look a little bleak,' admitted the Doctor. 'Perhaps the season hasn't started yet!'

Sarah was in no mood for jokes. 'Come on, Doctor, where are we?'

The Doctor picked up a chunk of rock.

'Well, it isn't peppermint, and it doesn't say Southend all the way through. Jurassic limestone, by the look of it. We appear to have landed in a quarry, Sarah. If we're lucky we might find some interesting fossils.'

A man in donkey jacket and protective helmet appeared on the cliff-top and stared in appalled surprise at the two figures below him. 'Hey, you,' he yelled. 'You two—look out! Get away from there!'

The wind caught his words and snatched them away.

The burly man's name was Tom Abbott, and he was foreman of the quarry's blasting crew. His safety record had been unblemished for twenty years, and he didn't intend to have it ruined now. He turned and ran back along the cliff edge. Over by the gate he could see Mike, his explosives engineer crouched over his detonating equipment.

Abbott waved his arms frantically, scissoring them above his head in a cutting gesture.

Mike nodded cheerfully, and reached for the handle of his detonator.

Abbott was frozen for a moment, realising his colleague's mistake, realising too that he was too far away to correct it. He turned and ran back to the quarry edge. 'You two—get away from there! We're *blasting* and you're right by the charges!'

For a moment the wind dropped and this time the Doctor heard him. He looked up and saw the frantically waving figure above them and suddenly realised what it was trying to tell them.

The Doctor's mind worked with terrific speed. No use just running blindly, they might well be going towards the hidden charges. There was a rocky overhang jutting out of the bottom of the cliff. 'Run, Sarah!' yelled the Doctor and began dragging her towards it.

Mike's hand came down on the plunger of the detonator ...

The Doctor heard the dull thump of the explosion and gave Sarah a frenzied shove, sending her stumbling beneath the overhang. With a shattering roar, half the cliff face erupted and came pouring down towards them. The Doctor was swept away by an avalanche of rocks ...

Tom Abbott ran desperately across the quarry floor. Much of the area was filled with rubble now, and the air was full of choking dust. He saw a tall figure lying face down at the edge of a pile of rocks. To his enormous relief, he saw it move and stumble coughing to its feet.

Immediately Abbott's relief was transformed to anger. 'How the blazes did you get down here? Didn't you see the signs, the flags? You must have heard the hooters! You've got no flaming right to be in this quarry in the first place ...' He broke off as the man rubbed a hand dazedly across his grimy forehead. 'Here, you all right?' said Abbott roughly. 'What about the girl?'

The Doctor was looking for the spur of rock. It was gone now, completely buried under the rock-fall.

'She must be under there ...'

Abbott heard a shout and looked up. A group of his men had reached the top of the cliff. He cupped his hands round his mouth. 'Accident! Someone buried. Get an ambulance right away—and get a squad down here with some gear ...'

He ran across to the Doctor who was busily heaving rocks away from the pile. He looked up as Abbott approached. 'She's under here somewhere, under the ledge. You remember there was a ledge, a kind of over-hang?'

'Let's hope she is under it,' said Abbott grimly. 'About fifty ton of rock on top of her if she isn't.'

The Doctor was hurling rocks from the pile with frantic speed. Abbott grabbed his arm and pulled him away. 'Hang about, hang about ...'

'But Sarah's under there.'

Men with picks and shovels were running down to-wards them. 'You'll have the rest of the cliff down on her going at it like that,' said Abbott. 'Leave it to my lads, they're experts.' He called to the approaching men. 'Get that stuff off the top there—she's under some kind of overhang. Take it easy, we don't want the whole lot caving in.'

The men began attacking the pile, shifting rocks away with amazing speed. Abbott drew the Doctor to one side. 'Come over here a minute.'

The Doctor's eyes were fixed on the working men. 'Yes, what is it?'

'Look, we'll do everything we can,' said Abbott awk-wardly. 'But if it turns out she is—done for, well, I'm not accepting any responsibility, not for myself, or for the company. I don't want to sound heartless, but you had no right to be in here, and me and my lads aren't carrying the can.'

Impatiently the Doctor pulled away. 'Yes, yes, all right, no one's blaming you. Now let's get on with it, shall we?'

He ran back to help the men on the rock pile.

Sarah awoke to darkness and confusion. Every bone in her body seemed to hurt, her head ached, and her lungs felt coated with dust. Worse still, she was trapped. She couldn't move. Faintly she could hear the sound of picks and shovels, feel the vibration in the rock. She was tucked under the overhanging ledge, and its protection had undoubtedly saved her life. The rubble had swept past burying the ledge entirely and now Sarah lay wedged in a sort of tiny cave. She struggled and managed to free her right arm, thrusting it into a gap in the rock just above her. 'Doctor, are you there?' she called feebly. 'I can't move ... my legs are stuck. Doctor, help me ...'

The hand groping above her touched something—something that felt curiously like another hand ... Sarah grabbed it and tried to pull herself free. The thing resisted briefly, and then came away, and Sarah slumped back with it in her hand.

She looked down and saw what she was holding and fainted.

The Doctor lifted away the last layer of rocks—and saw Sarah's face. Leaning forward, he got his ear close to her mouth. 'She's still breathing ...'

Carefully the rescue squad moved away the rest of

the rocks, and soon the Doctor and Abbott were able to free Sarah's body. As they lifted her free, they heard the siren of the approaching ambulance.

'What's that she's holding?' said Abbott suddenly.

The Doctor looked down. Sarah was clutching a fossilised stone hand.

2

The Ring of Power

The Doctor looked thoughtfully at the stone hand. 'She didn't have to go to those lengths!'

'What?'

'To find interesting fossils! Give it to me, will you?'

Abbott drew back. 'I'm not touching the thing.'

'Just hold her, then.' Abbott supported Sarah's weight while the Doctor attempted to take the stone hand away from her. It was surprisingly difficult. Sarah was gripping the hand with tremendous force, and the Doctor had to unclasp her fingers one by one. As he freed the hand, Sarah's fingers clenched and unclenched convulsively.

The Doctor stood holding the fossil, studying it absorbedly. It was a right hand, human, or at least humanoid in shape, rather large with long powerful fingers. The first finger was missing, and on the middle finger was a heavy ring, with a square-cut blue crystal. The Doctor tried to take it off but it was corroded on to the stone.

It was the ring that was really puzzling. Without it the hand could have been a fragment of some ancient statue. But the ring was real, not carved—and who would put a real jewel on a statue?

The Doctor was still studying the strange object when the ambulance men appeared. They took Sarah from Abbott and lifted her carefully on to a stretcher, covering her with a blanket. Suddenly Sarah began moaning and twisting. The hand that had held the fossil was still clenching and unclenching convulsively. On a sudden impulse the Doctor gave her back the fossil. Her fingers closed on it fiercely and she relaxed immediately, lying back as if asleep. The Doctor tucked the blanket round her and the ambulance men carried her away. The Doctor stood staring after her. 'You'd better go with her, mate,' said Abbott. 'Get yourself seen to as well.'

The Doctor realised that his hands were cut and bleeding, there was a bruise on his forehead, and by the feel of things a lot more all over his body. 'Yes, of course, you're quite right. Look, I wouldn't say anything about the fossil for the moment. I may want to talk to you later.'

'Oh, will you? Well, I shall want to talk to you as well, mate, coming in here and ...'

But the Doctor was already running after Sarah. The ambulance men were lifting her into the ambulance, which stood parked by the quarry entrance. He climbed in the back with her, and it drove away.

The Doctor sat patiently in a hospital cubicle while a keen young medical student cleaned the dirt and gravel from his cuts. 'Just superficial cuts and abrasions, nothing to worry about.'

'Ow!' The Doctor winced as the student plied his swab enthusiastically.

'Sorry, did I hurt you?'

'Oh no!'

'Wonderful thing, pain,' said the student solemnly. 'Without pain no race can survive.'

'I am well aware of that!' The Doctor winced again.

'It acts as a warning, you see, an autonomic defence mechanism.' With a final dab the student stepped back. 'There, all finished.'

'Thank you. Tell me, how's Miss Smith? Sarah Jane Smith, the girl I came in with?'

'Still unconscious, but there's no need to worry. There doesn't seem to be any serious injury.'

'Any signs of paralepsis?'

'Not as far as I know ...' The student registered the Doctor's use of the medical term.

'Are you a doctor yourself, by any chance?'

'Yes, of a sort.' The Doctor stood up.

The student smiled, pleased to find a colleague. 'That's interesting. Tell me, sir, where did you qualify?'

'A place called Gallifrey.'

'Don't think I've heard of it. It's not in England, is it?'

The Doctor shook his head.

'Ireland, perhaps?'

'Very probably. Look, could I see Miss Smith, do you think?'

'Certainly, Doctor. We'll go and have a look at her now.'

Sarah was in a small ward just down the corridor. She lay peacefully sleeping, a nurse straightening her pillows. The student looked down at her. 'Apparently she's still in shock.'

'Has she been given sedation?'

'No, only a simple anti-tetanus shot.'

'Anti-tetanus?'

'Yes. Just take a look at her right hand and forearm ...'

The Doctor lifted Sarah's right arm from beneath the bedclothes. The hand was clenched into a tight fist, the arm-muscles bunched and hard. 'You're right. It's as solid as stone ...'

'It's only in the hand and forearm. May be psychological reaction to stress. I gather she was clutching something very hard when she was brought in. Perhaps the muscles have locked in that position ...'

'Did you see the thing she was holding?'

'Some kind of fossil, I think. It was sent direct to Doctor Carter at the pathology lab.'

'How do I get there?'

'Turn left down the corridor and follow the signs.'

'Right, then, that's where I'll be. Let me know as soon as she comes round, will you?'

The stone hand lay in a white plastic tray on a bench in the cluttered pathology lab. The Doctor stood looking on while Doctor Carter bustled about. He was preparing a microscope slide containing a tiny sliver of stone scraped from the fossil. Carter placed the slide under the microscope and bent over the eyepiece. 'Curious object, Doctor. How did she come by it?'

'She found it in a quarry, just before she was hurt.'

Carter was a harassed-looking man with untidy grey hair.

'Well, it's interesting, most interesting—but we simply haven't the equipment to deal with it. The whole thing's completely baffling.'

The Doctor lifted a set of X-ray plates from a nearby bench. 'What do you make of these?'

'Not much! No tissue differentation, no blood, no muscle. No indication of a living organism whatsoever. You usually get some idea of structure from a fossil, but with this—nothing!'

'So it's really made of stone then, not a fossil at all? Part of a statue perhaps ...'

'That doesn't fit either. Take a look at this.'

The Doctor moved over to the microscope and looked through the eyepiece. The slide showed an intricate crystalline structure of unusual formation. 'It's beautiful ...' said the Doctor softly.

'Maybe it is—but it's got nothing to do with clinical pathology!'

'Does this crystalline lattice formation remind you of anything?'

'Well, it's not organic. You need a geologist, not a doctor!'

'I think it's silicone-based,' said the Doctor, almost to himself. 'Part of a living form with a silicon-based molecular infrastructure.'

Carter stared at him. 'A creature like that would be made of stone ... living stone!'

'Exactly!'

'Perhaps it's all some elaborate hoax,' suggested Carter hopefully. 'Medical students are always up to that kind of thing ...'

'I very much doubt it. Tell me, have we got access to an electron microscope?'

'There's one in Virology—if they'll part with it.'

'There was a ring on the hand when I first saw it. Did you take it off?'

'Someone else must have removed it before it got here.'

'Obviously. But when I tried the ring was corroded to the hand. I couldn't shift it ...' The Doctor considered the problem for a moment and then put it aside. 'I'll just go and get hold of that electron microscope. The Virology Department, you said?'

Sarah drifted gently back to consciousness. She was calm, smiling, completely relaxed. She slipped her right hand from beneath the covers and opened it. In her palm was the ring that had been on the hand. Sarah stared into the crystal. A strange blue fire seemed to flicker in its depths ...

Throwing back the blankets, Sarah sat up. She got out of bed, and opened the bedside locker that held her clothes.

To Carter's astonishment the Doctor returned in triumph, ushering before him two bewildered technicians wheeling a large and complex microscope. 'Over there, I think, gentlemen!'

The technicians began installing the microscope. Carter looked on in astonishment. 'You must have spun a very convincing story, Doctor. Virology usually hang on to that thing like grim death. What did you tell them?'

'I said we were investigating the possible viral infection of this planet by some organism from space.'

'Oh really, Doctor ... You're not serious?'

'Yes. Mind you, it's a fairly remote possibility. Viruses can survive for an incredibly long time, and under the most arduous conditions—but a hundred and fifty million years ...'

The technicians finished their installation, and the Doctor waved them away. 'Thank you, gentlemen. I'll let you know when I've finished with it.'

Carter looked at the stone hand in the tray. 'How do you know it's a hundred and fifty million years old?'

'When it was found it was embedded in a stratum of blackstone dolomite. Jurassic limestone.'

'And it'd been there for a hundred and fifty million years?'

'That's right.'

'But man didn't exist in Jurassic times!'

'That's true,' said the Doctor cheerfully. 'Look, would you be a good chap and prepare a slide for the electron microscope? I think I'd like to take a look at that quarry ...'

Fully dressed, the ring with the blue gem held in her right hand, Sarah opened the door and peeped into the corridor. A familiar figure turned the corner and came striding towards her. It was the Doctor. Sarah made no attempt to greet him. Instead she pulled the door to, and stood silently waiting.

The Doctor paused outside Sarah's room. He hesitated for a moment. Better to let her rest. He went on his way.

Sarah heard the footsteps move off, waited for a moment and then opened the door again. She slipped out into the empty corridor, heading in the direction from which the Doctor had just come.

Doctor Carter was bent over the eyepiece of the electron microscope, studying his newly prepared slide, when he heard movement behind him and straightened up.

An attractive dark-haired girl was taking the stone hand from its plastic tray. 'Hey, what do you think you're doing—oh, it's Miss Smith, isn't it? You're the one who found the thing . . .'

Sarah said nothing.

'I'll have to ask you to put that back, young lady. I'm helping your friend the Doctor to do some tests . . .'

Sarah raised her right hand in a curious pointing gesture. The blue crystal in the ring seemed to blaze and sparkle. 'Eldrad must live,' she said.

There was a bright blue flash from the ring and Carter crashed to the floor.

Ignoring him, Sarah looked round the laboratory until she found a plastic specimen box. She put the stone hand in the box and stood waiting.

Inside her head a voice said, 'Obey the will of Eldrad. None shall interfere. You know what you must do . . .'

Clutching the box, Sarah hurried from the room.

3

Power Source

'This is where we set the charges,' said Abbott. He pointed to the blast holes drilled in the rock. 'Your fossil must have been in this stratum here.'

Tom Abbott was being surprisingly co-operative. At first the Doctor's reception had been rather hostile, but his insistence that no one blamed Abbott for the accident and that Sarah was comparatively unhurt, and above all his production of a set of impressive credentials from some secret Government establishment called UNIT, had all combined to put Abbott in a more friendly frame of mind. He had even agreed to move the old blue police box, in which the Doctor stored his equipment, to a safe part of the quarry, and look after it until the Doctor had time to arrange for its removal.

The Doctor looked round. The loose rock had been carted away by now, and preparations for more blasting were under way. 'You found nothing in the rubble?'

Puzzled, Abbott shook his head. 'No ... What sort of thing are you looking for?'

'Oh, bits and pieces, this and that ...' said the Doctor vaguely. 'Anything unusual.'

Abbott shook his head. 'We get the odd fossil

26

occasionally, of course, but I've never seen anything like that hand ...'

'You didn't find any metal fragments? No plastic, nothing like that?'

'Plastic? You're joking!'

'Space vehicles tend to be made of metal, plastic or ceramic,' said the Doctor solemnly.

'Spaceships? All that time ago? Come on now ...'

'Life forms don't all reach the same stage of development at the same time, you know. Civilisations rise and fall, pass each other like ships in the universal night of the cosmos ...'

Abbott looked strangely at him, and cleared his throat. 'Well, I'd better let you get on with it then. Work to do myself ...' He turned to go but curiosity got the better of him. 'The feller that hand belonged to ... You reckon he copped it in some crash then, all that time ago?'

'I did at first, but now I'm not so sure. There should be some trace of the crash, a piece of wreckage, a fragment of anatomy ... But there's nothing ...'

'So it must be a fossil after all then?'

The Doctor looked up at the sky. 'Unless of course the hand just came floating down on its own, and fell plop into the primeval mud. But why? And where from? And where was it going to, eh? Tell me that!'

Tom Abbott had no answers for him.

Doctor Carter struggled slowly to his feet, trying to remember what had happened ... He felt weak and shaky all over, as if he'd had a massive electric shock.

Things began coming back to him. That girl ... He looked at the empty plastic tray that had held the hand ... Leaning against a bench he reached for the phone. 'Hullo, Reception. Have you seen that girl who was brought in earlier? Dark hair, some kind of striped overall dress ... She's taken something from my laboratory. If you see her, hold her and call the police.' He paused. 'What do you mean she left an hour ago, she's only just ...' Carter looked at his watch and registered the time. He'd been unconscious for over an hour. 'Good Lord! All right, thank you, never mind.' He put down the phone.

The Doctor opened the door of Sarah's room, and saw the empty bed. He crossed to the clothes locker and opened it. It too was empty. The Doctor turned and hurried from the room.

Doctor Carter was standing in the middle of the pathology lab, staring bewilderedly about him. 'Doctor Carter! Have you seen Miss Smith?'

'Yes, I have!' said Carter indignantly. 'She's stolen the hand! Tell me, does she usually go around knocking people out like that? Just as I was getting somewhere, too.'

'What happened?'

Carter frowned. 'I'm not sure ... I was at the 'scope. She came in. She said—someone must live, there was a flash, and I can't remember any more.'

'She hit you?'

'I suppose she must have done. Though I was here, and she was by the door ... I'm afraid I'll have to put the police on to it.'

'Yes, I suppose so,' agreed the Doctor absently. He was staring at the empty tray.

'Did you find anything at the quarry?'

'Negative evidence, you might say. No fragments, so whatever it was didn't crash.' The Doctor peered through the eyepiece of the electron microscope. 'But there was an explosion of some kind,' he said excitedly. 'Look, you can see the fracture lines on your sample ...'

'But if there was an explosion, it must have been millions of years ago ...'

The Doctor nodded. 'And millions of miles away, probably. Fascinating, isn't it?'

'Perhaps it is. But it still doesn't explain why your Miss Smith should want the hand.'

'Perhaps the hand wanted Miss Smith!'

Carter looked at him in baffled astonishment. 'What?'

'She's the only person who was in contact with it for any length of time. Probably the only living organism to be in contact with it since the explosion.'

'But it was petrified,' protested Carter. 'It was totally inert. Dead!'

'Inert, yes. But dead—I think not.'

Carter wandered over to the electron microscope. 'I thought I detected some strange type of subatomic structure in the crystal formation. Bit like a double helix, you know, the DNA molecule ...' He peered into the eyepiece. 'Good grief!'

'What is it?'

'It's changed. The entire crystalline structure has

changed while we've been talking!'

The Doctor took Carter's place at the eyepiece, and studied the sample intently. 'I think your sample has been quietly absorbing radiation from this machine.'

'Absorbing radiation?'

'Yes. It's regenerating. The fracture lines have vanished. And if that's the case, the hand will be looking for another power source . . .' The Doctor straightened up. 'Tell me, Doctor Carter—where's the nearest nuclear reactor?'

The Experimental Atomic Energy Complex sprawled over several miles of English countryside. Devoted to work on new and experimental types of reactor, the secluded area was surrounded by a high wire fence and patrolled by armed security guards at all times.

Sarah Jane Smith arrived at the main gate, still clutching the specimen box that contained the stone hand. Above the gate a huge sign read:

EXPERIMENTAL NUCLEAR RESEARCH
AND DEVELOPMENT ESTABLISHMENT
NO UNAUTHORISED ENTRY

Ignoring the sign, Sarah walked straight through the open gate. An armed security guard hurried forward to bar her way. Sarah raised the crystal ring. There was a blinding flash from the blue gemstone and the guard staggered back and fell. Sarah walked past his body and into the Research Complex.

Soon she was passing through a metal forest of

gleaming coolant towers and domed reactor housings. High above her walkways and gantries stretched in every direction like the streets of some futuristic city, but Sarah paid no attention to her surroundings. Unerringly she picked her way through the maze of buildings towards her destination.

Carter was a vintage car enthusiast and in the car park he led the Doctor to an old but powerful Bentley. Carter was something of an amateur racing driver too, and they took off from the car park with a spurt of gravel and a satisfying roar. Soon the car was speeding along the road that led to the atomic research establishment.

Much of the research area was semi-automated, and once past the perimeter guard Sarah saw no one on her way to the group of reactors that formed the heart of the complex. Unseen, she crossed the turbine hall, and climbed a metal ladder that led up to the heating platform. She crossed this too, and soon she was crossing the wide metal walkway that led to the main reactor.

She opened a heavy metal blast door, and entered the building.

Since there had been no outcry and no alarm, it wasn't until the relief guard appeared that the duty guard's unconscious body was found. The guard stared down at his colleague for a moment, then turned and ran for the gatehouse.

*

By now Sarah was well inside number four reactor. A glowing sign in the corridor read, 'CONDITION TWO: DANGER.' She hurried on.

As Carter's car roared up to the main gate of the complex, the Doctor spotted the sprawled body of the guard and knew he'd found what he was looking for. He pointed and Carter brought the car to a screeching halt.

The Doctor jumped out of the car, heaved up the barrier and jumped back in the car as Carter drove into the complex. Rifle-carrying guards appeared from every side and a warning shot rang over their heads. The nearest guard yelled, 'Halt! Halt or we fire!'

Carter stopped the car and the ring of armed men ran to surround them.

The Doctor sighed.

Still moving at the same steady pace, her face blank and calm, Sarah walked through the central reactor hall. Now the warning notices read:

RADIATION CONDITION SIX
EXTREME HAZARD

A technician appeared at the top of a metal staircase, looking like some alien astronaut in his protective suit and helmet. He looked unbelievingly at the incongruous figure of the girl with the box and clattered down the steps towards her, desperately waving her away from the hall. Sarah raised the ring, there was a flash, and the technician fell. Sarah walked past his body and began climbing the staircase.

Her final destination was the short, wide corridor that led into the heart of the atomic pile. It ended in a thick lead-shielded door bearing one word in huge red letters. 'FISSION!'

Sarah spun the wheel-locks that freed the door. As she pulled the door open the reactor's warning system erupted in protest. Lights flashed and bells rang all over the complex. A voice began booming from the loudspeakers. 'EMERGENCY. ALL PERSONNEL PROCEED IMMEDIATELY TO SAFE AREAS. EMERGENCY SQUAD TO MAIN REACTOR PILE. THIS IS NOT AN EXERCISE, REPEAT, THIS IS NOT AN EXERCISE!'

The din was fantastic, but Sarah didn't seem to hear it. She heaved open the door and entered the fission control room, closing the door behind her.

Immediately she was inside the room, the box in her hand started to pulse with life. She raised the lid.

The hand was throbbing and glowing. As Sarah watched, the missing third finger grew into existence before her eyes. The hand had regenerated itself.

Inside the box the hand began to *move*, twisting and flexing as it returned to life ...

4

The Will of Eldrad

Sarah stood clasping the box, looking down at the pulsing, flexing hand within. Her head was cocked a little to one side. It was as though the hand was talking to her ...

Professor Owen Watson, Director of the Research Complex, was a burly, tough-looking irascible man whose appearance suggested the rugby field rather than the laboratory. At the moment he was standing by the central computer in the middle of the main control room, glaring about him like an angry bull about to charge.

There was panic and pandemonium all around. The racket of the alarm system blared from the loud-speakers and at the control banks that lined the big semi-circular control room, agitated technicians were close to panic as they studied their instrument readings with alarm.

The Director threw back his head and bellowed, 'CAN WE LOSE SOME OF THE NOISE IN HERE?'

From the other side of the room, Driscoll, his number two, shouted, 'Sorry, sir, can't hear you!'

Professor Watson groaned. He saw his personal

assistant, the cool, blonde, imperturbable Miss Jackson, moving calmly through the chaos. 'MISS JACKSON!' bawled Watson. 'GET THIS DAMN RACKET STOPPED, WILL YOU? I CAN'T HEAR MYSELF THINK!'

'I'm doing my best, Director,' said Miss Jackson reprovingly. She crossed to a wall-panel and began flicking cut-off switches. Bells stopped ringing and the clangour of the sirens died away. The noise could still be heard from outside the control room, but at least it was muted by distance. The Director gave a groan of relief. 'Now perhaps we can find out what's going on here ...'

The Doctor and Carter were being marched along the corridor by two armed guards. The fact that they'd been found on the scene of the crime, so to speak, had made their captors hostile and suspicious, and no one would listen to the Doctor's explanations. The guards were sticking to their orders. Any intruders were to be taken to the Security area for questioning.

A voice blared out from a nearby loudspeaker. 'All personnel proceed immediately to safe areas. This is not an exercise. All personnel to safe areas immediately!'

The two guards exchanged worried looks. They were moving away from the shelter area. They hesitated for a moment, then marched on with the prisoners.

A group of white-coated technicians came running

along the corridor towards them, jostling in panic to get by. For a moment the corridor was jammed with struggling figures. 'Where do you think you're going?' shouted one of the technicians. 'Can't you hear the alarm? Get to the shelters!'

The technicians forced their way past, and when they moved on the guards suddenly realised they were alone. Their prisoners had vanished! They looked round wildly, then ran off after the vanishing technicians.

A door in the corridor opened, and the Doctor and Carter peered cautiously out. 'What do you think you're doing?' demanded Carter. 'We could have been shot!'

The Doctor grinned. 'But we weren't, were we? They were glad of the excuse to turn back!'

Carter started to move off after the others. 'Come on, Doctor, this way out.'

'No, this way in!' The Doctor set off in the opposite direction.

Carter hurried after him. 'Where now?'

'To the main control room ...'

'Yes,' said Sarah. 'Yes, I understand.' She closed the lid of the box and put it down carefully on the floor. She crossed to the fission room door and began bolting it from the inside.

The control room technicians were still chatting agitatedly. Professor Watson slammed down the telephone and turned round. 'Quiet please, everyone,' called Miss Jackson. No one heard her.

Professor Watson bellowed. 'Can we have silence in here?' Then abandoning politeness, he bellowed, 'Will you all shut up, please? SHUT UP!'

The babble of voices died away. Watson crossed to the communications console. 'I'm about to make an announcement to the Complex. The rest of you had better listen.' He turned to the microphone. 'Attention all personnel, this is the Director. We have an emergency in the experimental reactor in Section Four. It appears to be an act of deliberate sabotage.' He paused to gather his thoughts. This had to be put carefully if he was to avoid a panic. 'Some unfortunate young woman, probably a lunatic, has infiltrated the complex. She has knocked out two of the security personnel and locked herself in the fission control room, next to the reactor core. It may well be an act of suicidal protest by a member of some extremist group. On the other hand it is possible that she's a terrorist with the knowledge to render the pile critical and destroy this entire establishment. We are going ahead with an emergency shutdown, and we'll do our best to get her out before she does any real damage. All personnel are to remain in their safety shelters. If necessary, evacuation instructions will be issued later. That is all.'

All over the complex grave-faced men listened to Professor Watson's voice in a stunned silence. They were used to working with the remote possibility of atomic explosion, but so elaborate were the safety measures, so automatic the protective routines, that

37

the thought of any real danger had long been pushed to the back of their minds. The complex as a whole contained not one but a whole series of nuclear reactors. If one of them should blow and set off a chain reaction ...

In the control room, Watson mopped his brow, and issued a steady stream of instructions for the emergency shut-down of all the reactors in the area. There was a burst of frantic activity from the technicians, who were suddenly too busy to be frightened.

Watson stood supervising the controlled confusion, while Miss Jackson checked the progress reports as they came in. Finally, she said, 'The shut-down of the other reactors is proceeding according to plan, sir, but we're getting no response from the neutron core of number four reactor.'

'Which means she knows enough about it to do some damage,' said Watson grimly. 'Mr Driscoll, get some men suited up and armed and get her out of there!'

'Yes, sir. I'll see to it right away.'

At this point the Doctor and Carter appeared and hurried across the busy room towards Watson. He stared at them in astonishment. 'Who the devil are you two?'

'You must be the Director of this establishment,' said the Doctor politely. 'How do you do? I'm the Doctor, and this is Doctor Carter.'

Watson was about to explode when Carter said hurriedly, 'We're from the hospital, you see. This girl escaped—we think she may have come here.'

'She's here all right—inside one of my reactors. Hospital, you said? She's an escaped lunatic then?'

'She's certainly not quite herself at the moment,' said the Doctor wryly.

'She must be mad,' said Watson. 'Stark staring mad. You're welcome to have her back as soon as we can get our hands on her. Meanwhile, I've got an emergency on my hands.'

'Have you tried talking to her? Perhaps I could have a word ...'

'This is no time for the bedside manner, Doctor,' said Watson witheringly. 'Now stay out of my way. Better still, get out of here altogether.'

The Doctor wandered over to Miss Jackson, who was standing by the central computer. 'Would you be good enough to punch up plans of the building, please?'

Something about the calm authority of his manner made Miss Jackson obey. 'Yes, sir.' She went to the computer keyboard, and a complex plan sprang up on the computer's read-out screen.

There came an angry bellow from the Director. 'Miss Jackson!'

'Excuse me, sir.' Miss Jackson moved away.

The Doctor stood studying the plans. His long fingers flicked over the keyboard and the plan began appearing in a series of magnified sections. The Doctor began memorising them, one by one, until the layout of the entire building was fixed in his mind ...

Clumsy in their all-enveloping radiation suits, the security guards wrestled with the fission room door. It refused to shift. Even when they brought tools and tried to force it, the door wouldn't budge. It was as if some invisible force was holding it closed. Finally Driscoll waved the others away, and went back to the control room to report his failure.

'No good?' said Watson indignantly. 'What do you mean, no good?'

'The manual locks seem to be jammed,' said Driscoll wearily. 'We just can't get past the fission room door.'

The Doctor looked up for a moment, then went back to memorising the plans.

'What's our shut-down situation now?' demanded Watson. Miss Jackson consulted her clipboard. 'Everything's closed down except number four reactor now, sir, the one the girl's in. The controls still aren't responding.'

'What sort of radiation levels are we getting in there?'

Driscoll was studying a set of dials. 'According to this, she's soaking up enough radiation to kill a herd of elephants. She must be dead by now.'

'I very much doubt it,' said the Doctor. 'Why don't you at least *try* talking to her? Surely you've got some kind of audio-visual link?'

'I thought I told you to get out of here,' said Watson irritably. But he moved to a monitor screen and stabbed at the controls. After a moment, a blurred picture of Sarah appeared. She was standing perfectly still, as if waiting for something. 'You in the fission room,' growled Watson. 'Can you hear me?'

'Her name's Smith,' said the Doctor helpfully. 'Sarah Jane Smith.'

'Now listen, Miss Smith,' shouted Watson. 'Your life is in danger, and you are endangering the lives of hundreds of others. Now what is it you want?'

The figure on the screen did not move or speak.

'Let me talk to her,' said the Doctor.

'Try if you like—but I don't think she'll listen.'

'Radiation level in there's still rising, Professor,' said Driscoll. 'Nothing we can do to check it—she seems to have put some sort of lock on the controls.'

Watson sighed. The girl seemed young and pretty, and for all the trouble she was causing, he couldn't help feeling sorry for her. 'Well, she's had it now. She can't survive in there much longer.' Watson turned his attention to more urgent problems. 'If the radiation level keeps on rising that reactor's going to go up —and there's nothing we can do to stop it. You'd better start full evacuation alert, Miss Jackson. Every living person in a twelve mile radius. And inform Whitehall ...'

Watson issued a series of complicated instructions which Miss Jackson noted down with her usual calm efficiency. She moved to the communications console, and Watson turned to the Doctor, who was addressing the silent figure on the screen. 'Sarah! Sarah, can you hear me?' There was no reply.

'Told you she wouldn't listen,' grumbled Watson. 'Now then, Doctor, will you kindly get out of here?'

Suddenly Sarah spoke. 'It is no use.' Everyone crowded round the monitor screen.

'Sarah!' said the Doctor urgently. 'Sarah, listen to me ...'

'Eldrad must live. There is nothing more to say.

Eldrad must live.'

Doctor Carter was standing at the back of the little crowd. Sarah's eyes seemed to be staring from the screen, straight into his own. For some reason he remembered the smooth, warm feeling of the stone hand when he'd held it to prepare the slide ... Suddenly Sarah's words seemed to contain some great truth, something he'd always known but had now realised for the first time. A voice spoke inside Carter's head. *'Eldrad must live!'*

'Eldrad must live,' whispered Carter.

He started edging closer to the Doctor.

5

Eldrad Must Live

Professor Watson glared at the screen. 'What's she talking about?'

'Sssh!' said the Doctor reprovingly.

'Eldrad must live,' said Sarah again.

(Behind them Carter, unseen, was mouthing the words in silent agreement.)

'Sarah, who is Eldrad?'

'Some political assassin, no doubt,' muttered Watson. 'One of her fellow terrorists!'

'Will you be quiet, man?' snapped the Doctor. 'Sarah, who is Eldrad?'

Sarah began to chant, 'Eldrad must live. Eldrad, the creator, the saviour. Eldrad must live.'

The Doctor moved away from the screen. 'Keep her talking. Try to distract her attention. I'm going in there.'

Watson stared at him. 'How? The doors are jammed.'

The Doctor pointed to the plan on the computer read-out screen. 'According to this there's a cooling duct leading directly into the fission chamber.'

Driscoll came and studied the plan. 'But the outlet's high on the cooling tower. You'd never reach it. And even if you did, do you realise the temperature in there? You'll roast, man!'

The Doctor grinned. 'Not if I move quickly enough!' He headed for the door.

Carter hurried after him. 'I'll come with you.'

The Doctor spoke over his shoulder. 'It's all right, Doctor Carter, there's no need.'

The voice inside Carter's head spoke again. 'Go with him. *She* may need help.' Carter ran after the Doctor.

In the fission control room red lights were flashing, alarm bells ringing, and dial after dial was registering 'critical'. Sarah ignored all these danger signs, attentive only to the voice inside her head. 'It is the law. Eldrad must live!' She stared intently at the box, nodded obediently, then crossed to the video communications set-up in the corner. She raised her hand, the ring flashed——

(In the main control room, the vision screen went blank. 'Damn!' said Watson furiously. 'What am I supposed to do now?')

Sarah went back to the box, opened it and stood waiting. The stone hand began climbing crab-like out of the box ...

The Doctor picked his way through the gleaming maze of domes, towers and walkways, stopped at the base of an enormous silver cooling tower and pointed upwards. 'We have to climb to the top of this and cross that walkway to the adjoining tower to reach the cooling duct exit.'

44

Carter too stared upwards. The slender tower rose to a dizzying height, and the walkway was no more than a thin metal ladder.

'Sure you want to come?' asked the Doctor.

Carter nodded silently.

There was a narrow ladder bolted to the side of the tower.

The Doctor began to climb.

Carter followed him up the ladder, a few rungs behind.

Miss Jackson was talking into a telephone. 'It seems to be some kind of slogan,' she said calmly. 'It could be a person or a political organisation, we just don't know. You might see if Special Branch has got anything ... Yes, that's right, Eldrad. E-L-D-R-A-D ...'

Professor Watson was still flicking at the microphone switch. 'Hello, Miss Smith ... Can you hear me, Miss Smith? Oh, blast the girl! What's she doing in there?'

The warning dials in the fission control room had already moved past the danger sector. They were now in the 'critical' red sector, the last stage before an actual explosion.

Sarah was watching the hand. It had crawled across the floor to a heavy metal door set into the far wall. This door gave on to the live core of the reactor. Unless the reactor was completely closed down it was death to enter it, even in a radiation suit. The door was held closed by a complex array of safety bolts, and a combination lock. Sarah began to open the bolts one by one.

The hand crouched at her feet like a giant spider, scuttling impatiently to and fro . . .

The Doctor reached the top of the ladder at last and hung there gasping for breath. Wind tugged at his clothing and fluttered his scarf.

Below him, Carter struggled painfully up the ladder until his head was level with the Doctor's feet.

'This is the tricky bit,' yelled the Doctor. 'We've got to cross the connecting ladder to the next tower, then swing down into that cooling duct.' He pointed to an opening just below the connecting ladder on the other side.

Carter nodded grimly, his face pale, his mind in the grip of the alien will.

The Doctor climbed on to the horizontal ladder and began crawling slowly across. Carter followed him.

Miss Jackson put down the phone and turned to Professor Watson. 'Special Branch say they've no record of any person or organisation by the name of Eldrad, sir. Nothing from Intelligence either.'

Professor Watson nodded indifferently. He'd forgotten he'd even asked for the check, and it didn't seem very important anyway—not with every dial in sector four well into the 'critical' zone.

'Shouldn't we be leaving, sir?' asked Miss Jackson gently. Everyone else had already left, and they were alone in the control room. The entire building had been evacuated and there was eerie silence.

Professor Watson looked round. 'Yes, thank you, Miss Jackson. You can go now.'

'What about you, sir?'

'Somebody's got to stay in the control room while there's still a chance to do anything. Who knows, that girl may come to her senses, or the Doctor may reach her in time. While there's still a chance I can do something ...'

'I'd like to stay, sir.'

'No. You'll leave at once, please. That's an order, Miss Jackson.' Watson's voice was curiously calm for such a bad-tempered man.

Miss Jackson looked at him for a moment, then said quietly, 'Yes, sir,' just as she'd done so many times before. Gathering up her notes she walked unhurriedly from the control room.

Her footsteps died away, and Professor Watson looked round the empty control room. Suddenly he realised that the phones were still working. He could call his wife and children—one last time ...

Sarah freed the last bolt on the metal door and tried to tug it open. It refused to move. The complex combination lock still held it closed. She looked down at the glowing, pulsing hand at her feet, listened and then nodded. She began to move the combination dial to and fro. Looking at the hand for instructions, she dialled, waited, then dialled again ...

Professor Watson's little daughter had answered the phone. Delighted to find her father on the line she'd began a long rambling account of some school triumph. For a moment Watson felt like yelling at her to get off the line. Then he thought it would be a pity if his daughter's last memory was of him shouting at her. He forced himself to listen patiently, then said, 'That's very good, Susy, I'm sure your teacher was pleased. Be a good girl and get mum for me, will you? I'm a bit short of time. Quickly now.'

When his wife came on the line, Watson found himself quite incapable of telling her that he would probably be dead in a few minutes time. Let her be happy for a while longer, she'd hear soon enough. Instead he said cheerfully, 'Hullo, love, it's me. I'm afraid I've got to stay a bit later than usual tonight, there's a bit of a crisis. Just thought I'd let you know where I was. Yes, I'll see you later then. Bye, love.'

He put down the phone. The dials for sector four had moved into the final unlabelled black sector. He remembered an old technician's joke. 'When you see the dial in the black—you're already dead . . .'

The Doctor was halfway across the connecting ladder, Carter crawling close behind him. The slender metal bridge was bending ominously beneath their combined weights, and the Doctor wondered if he ought to have insisted they crossed one at a time. Still, too late to worry about that now . . . Decent of Carter to insist on coming with him like that. Curious too, the man was clearly terrified of heights.

The Doctor glanced down at the ground, a long, sickening distance below. A drop like that was enough to scare anyone. Come to think of it, he didn't much care for it himself. Hurriedly raising his eyes, he crawled on.

Carter was close behind him, the compulsion that filled his mind stronger than his fear of heights, and his distrust of the thin, swaying ladder. 'Eldrad must live,' said the voice in his mind. 'Nothing and no one must interfere. Obey the will of Eldrad. You know what you must do.'

Two thirds of the way across the ladder-bridge the Doctor paused to rewind his scarf, which was showing a disturbing tendency to get tangled between his legs. As he stopped, he saw Carter was still crawling on, getting too close to him for comfort. The Doctor waved him back, but Carter still came on, his face intent.

'Too scared to stop, poor chap,' thought the Doctor. Then Carter reached out, caught the trailing end of the Doctor's scarf and gave it a savage yank. The scarf tightened chokingly round the Doctor's neck. Carter heaved again, and the Doctor fell ...

6

Countdown

The Doctor reached upwards, grabbing wildly ... First one hand and then the other caught the rungs of the connecting-ladder, and he hung over the abyss below, swinging like a pendulum.

Carter frowned. His task was not yet complete. He crawled closer to the Doctor and stared down at him through the ladder rungs. 'Eldrad must live,' he whispered, and began prising the Doctor's fingers from the ladder-rungs one by one.

'Carter, what do you think you're doing?' howled the Doctor.

'It is the law. Eldrad must live. There must be no interference with his design. Eldrad must live!'

'So must I, I'm afraid,' said the Doctor determinedly. Abandoning any attempt to get back up on the ladder quickly, he began swinging hand over hand along the rungs to the other side.

Carter saw the Doctor disappearing, and made a desperate attempt to pull him back. But he was too late, the Doctor was already out of reach. The force of his lunge cost Carter his own balance, and he swayed and fell screaming from the ladder ...

The Doctor heard the scream, and twisted round. He saw the sprawling figure becoming smaller, smaller as it plummeted down, and struck the ground far below with a distant thud. The Doctor winced and turned away. He was sorry about Carter's fate, but he had problems of his own.

The end of the cooling duct was a few feet below him in the side of the tower. It was a large oval-shaped opening rather like the funnel on a ship. It was surrounded by smooth polished metal—there would be nowhere to grip if he missed his jump. The Doctor began swinging to and fro like an acrobat on the trapeze. At the end of his final swing he let go, shot feet first into the cooling duct and disappeared from sight.

The slope of the giant tube was very steep and the Doctor whizzed forwards as if on some mad helter skelter, gathering speed all the time. The metal of the duct was hot to the touch, and he was shooting downwards through a blast of hot air. It was like sliding down a chimney with the fire still going, and the Doctor's only hope was that he was moving too quickly to get badly burned ...

Sarah heard the final click and knew that the door was now unlocked. She reached for the handle and was about to pull it open when a metal grille above her head burst from off the wall and the Doctor shot out like the demon king in a pantomime. The end of his scarf was smouldering, and his clothes were smoking with the heat.

As the Doctor landed, Sarah raised the ring. Before she could blast him down the Doctor gasped, 'Eldrad must live!'

Sarah hesitated, puzzled to hear the commandment that ruled her brain from this unexpected source. Could it be that the Doctor wasn't an enemy after all?

The second of hesitation was all the Doctor needed. 'Eldrad must live,' he said again, and moved closer. His fist flashed out and Sarah went limp.

'Sorry about that,' said the Doctor and caught her falling body, lowering it gently to the ground.

Turning to the control console, the Doctor put in several minutes' furious activity. With Sarah unconscious, the will of the mysterious Eldrad lacked a channel, and the controls responded normally. As soon as he was finished, the Doctor picked up Sarah and carried her from the room.

He didn't notice the stone hand which had scuttled rat-like behind the console and was laying there motionless. Nor did he notice that as he carried Sarah from the room the crystal ring dropped from her hand and rolled into a corner.

Alone in the control room, Professor Watson sat at the main control console, his face lit up by the fierce flashing of a red warning light. He felt curiously calm. In a way he supposed he was making a futile gesture, going up with his reactor like a captain going down with his ship ... Yet somehow there didn't seem to be any choice. The entire experimental section was his responsibility, and if he could do nothing to prevent the catastrophe, then he must stay and take the consequences.

He looked dully at the flashing orange light—then suddenly jumped up. Orange! The light had changed to orange! The reactor was moving out of the red sector.

Watson jumped up and ran to the console that controlled section four. Indicator needles were swinging steadily across the dials, out of the black, down through the red, the yellow, and into the blue sector that meant 'normal', and finally to 'off'. Watson ran to the computer and punched up a request for a status report. The letters on the screen read, 'EMERGENCY SHUT-DOWN PROCEEDING.' Watson watched in astonishment as the news of the various shut-down stages flowed across the screen, concluding with the words, 'EMERGENCY SHUT-DOWN COMPLETE.'

He sank slowly into a seat trying to come to terms with the astonishing fact that he was still alive.

The Doctor's voice crackled from a loudspeaker. 'Professor Watson, can you hear me?'

'Doctor? Is that you?'

'Yes. Is everything under control now?'

'It seems to be. Where are you? And what about that girl, is she still alive?'

'Very much so. We're in decontamination.'

'I'll be down as soon as I've sorted things out. Well done, Doctor!'

Watson switched the speaker to the loudspeaker channel. 'Attention all personnel, this is the Director. The reactor in section four is now under control and the emergency is over. Please return to your posts.' A thought struck him. 'Oh, and will video maintenance please check the monitoring system for number four fission control room.'

Sarah lay stretched out on a couch in the decontamination area, while the Doctor hovered over her with a geiger counter, moving the instrument slowly up and down the length of her body. There was only the faint regular beep of the instrument ticking over, and the indicator needle was on the bottom register. The Doctor tapped the instrument like a man with a faulty barometer, and tried again. Still nothing. Sarah must have undergone a massive, possibly fatal exposure to radiation—yet the instrument showed that her body was radiation-free.

Sarah moaned, struggling to sit up. 'It's my legs, Doctor, I can't move. I'm trapped ...'

'It's all right, Sarah. You're safe now.'

She opened her eyes and looked dazedly around her. 'What happened? Am I in hospital?'

'Well, something like that.'

'Thank goodness. I was buried, Doctor, buried alive ...'

'What's the last thing you remember?'

Sarah rubbed her hand across her face, and winced. 'My chin hurts ...'

The Doctor coughed. 'Yes, well, never mind that. What's the last thing you remember?'

'There was a hand,' said Sarah slowly. 'Someone held out a hand to me. I thought it was you ... then, when I touched it, it was cold. I thought you'd been killed ... Then I must have passed out ...'

'Do you remember us digging you out? Going to the hospital? Seeing Doctor Carter?'

Sarah shook her head.

'Do you remember finding a fossil? A stone hand?'

'What on earth are you talking about, Doctor?'

The door was flung open and suddenly the room was crowded. There was Professor Watson, Miss Jackson, and behind them Driscoll, still wearing his radiation suit and carrying the protective helmet.

Watson loomed threateningly over Sarah. 'Now then, my girl, what the devil did you think you were doing?'

Sarah, who couldn't remember doing anything, stared at him in astonishment, and looked enquiringly up at the Doctor.

'Just a minute, Professor Watson,' said the Doctor. 'It's no use shouting at Sarah, she doesn't remember anything.'

'Very convenient!'

'It's all a bit more complicated than it might seem ...'

'Complicated? Do you realise we came close to a major nuclear disaster?'

'I'm well aware of that—but I don't think we can blame Miss Smith.'

'Now look here, Doctor, I realise you're trying to protect your patient, but diminished responsibility or not, she walked straight into the reactor room and——'

'How on earth did you get her out, Doctor?' asked Driscoll. 'The radiation in there ...'

The Doctor was tired of being badgered. 'If you'll all be quiet, I'll come to that in a moment.' Raising the geiger counter, he passed it over Sarah's body. 'Take a look at those readings. No trace of radioactivity whatsoever.'

'But that's impossible,' spluttered Driscoll. 'She was exposed to enough direct radiation to kill her instantly.'

'Exactly. But here she is, absolutely unharmed.'

Sarah was getting fed up with everyone talking over her head as though she was an invalid, a lunatic, and apparently some kind of criminal as well. She sat up and said firmly, 'Excuse me, but I gather all this involves me?'

The Doctor smiled down at her. 'I'm afraid it does, Sarah.'

'Then would somebody tell me what I'm supposed to have done?'

Driscoll shook his head in amazement. '*Supposed* to have done?'

'Actually, Doctor, I think we'd all like a full explanation,' said Professor Watson grimly.

'Well, I'll do my best. But I warn you, you won't believe it.' The Doctor hung up the geiger counter. 'To start with, I'm afraid Doctor Carter's dead. He died because he tried to kill me.'

There was a stunned silence.

The Doctor sighed. 'I think I'd better begin at the beginning.'

'Good idea,' said Sarah.

The Doctor gave her a reproving look. 'It all started when we found a stone hand in a quarry. Well, actually, you found it, Sarah ...'

The hand scurried across the floor of the fission room to the door of the atomic pile and hurled itself up towards the handle. It fell short, and dropped back to the floor. Again and again it tried, but always it fell short. Finally it abandoned the attempt and lay still, getting its strength ...

'And there you are,' concluded the Doctor. 'You just kept on saying "Eldrad must live".' By now they were back in the main control room. Sarah had refused to stay in bed, insisting she was perfectly well, and as Professor Watson felt he ought to be keeping an eye on things, they had all gone with him.

Sarah stared at the Doctor. '"Eldrad must live." I really said that?'

'You did. In fact you wouldn't say anything else.'

'This Eldrad,' said Watson thoughtfully. 'This—hand. It absorbed all the radiation and left Miss Smith unharmed?'

'More or less. It seems to need radiation much as we do oxygen.'

'Then you're saying it's a living thing?'

'Not just living, but growing, Professor. Regenerating!'

An internal phone rang, and Miss Jackson answered it. She turned to the director. 'Video maintenance, sir. They say the fission room monitor is working again. There should be a picture coming up now.'

They all crowded round the little monitor screen as it flickered into life. A whirling snowstorm effect cleared into a view of the fission room—and of the hand hurling itself desperately at the metal door.

'Incredible,' said Watson slowly. Then he pulled himself together. He was a scientist, and facts were facts, however unlikely. The hand was there, and it had to be dealt with. 'The first thing to do is get it out of there and put it into some sort of shielded container.'

The Doctor nodded his agreement. 'Right. Then we can study it, see what makes it tick.'

Driscoll said, 'I'll do it, sir. I'm already suited up.' He hurried from the room.

The Doctor started to follow him but Watson held him back. 'I'd rather have you up here, Doctor. Besides, you've been in there once, better not take chances.'

Driscoll went to the supply section and armed himself with a set of handling tongs and a shielded box. Then he made his way to section four and cautiously entered the fission room.

To his relief the hand had stopped scrabbling about and was lying quietly by the door of the fission chamber. He picked it up and dropped it into the shielded box, closing the lid.

Watching on the monitor screen, Watson gave a sigh of relief. 'Good, he's got it. He'll bring it to decontamination, we can meet him there.'

The camera's vision field didn't include the fission room entrance. They didn't see Driscoll pause by the threshold and stare down at something that lay at his feet.

Driscoll stared down at the ring. As he looked at it the blue crystal glowed fiercely. Driscoll bent and picked it up. Moved by some powerful compulsion he took off his gauntlet, and slipped the ring on his finger.

Inside his head a voice said, 'Eldrad must live!'

7

Blow-up

The hand lay motionless on a bench in the decontamination section. It might have been a fragment of some ancient statue being studied by a group of archaeologists—though archaeologists don't often use geiger counters.

The Doctor was moving the instrument all around the hand. 'You see? No radiation. It's absorbing the energy and using it to build tissue. The broken finger has already been regenerated.' He hung up the geiger counter. 'We'd better lock it away from any further energy source while we make up our minds what to do with it.'

Driscoll hurried forward. 'I'll see to it, sir.' He carried the hand away.

'Careful,' warned Sarah. 'It's not as harmless as it looks!'

'This ring, Sarah,' said the Doctor. 'The one you used on Carter and the guards . . . Where is it now?'

'I've no idea. I don't even know what you're talking about.'

'You had it in your hand.'

'Sorry, I just don't remember. Perhaps I dropped it.'

'Then it must still be in the reactor room.' The Doctor turned to Driscoll. 'Do you remember seeing a crystal ring with a big blue stone?'

Driscoll shook his head, his face strangely expressionless. 'I didn't see anything like that, sir.'

(Inside his mind a voice said, 'Eldrad must live.')

Driscoll said brightly, 'Shall I go and have a look for it, Doctor?'

'Would you mind? Maybe she dropped it when I dragged her out.'

Professor Watson made for the door. 'All right, Driscoll, you go ahead. I'll contact you from the control room.'

Watson and Driscoll left, and the Doctor closed the door behind them. 'Sit down, please, Sarah.'

Sarah perched on the edge of the bench and looked warily at the Doctor.

He came across to her, his eyes open very wide. 'Now then, Sarah, I want you to concentrate.'

'Oh, no, Doctor, not that again! That's not fair!' Sarah hated being hypnotised.

The Doctor reached out and touched her temple, and Sarah relaxed, staring into space.

In the same soothing voice the Doctor said, 'Now, tell me about Eldrad.'

'Eldrad must live,' said Sarah. 'We must obey.'

'We?' asked the Doctor sharply. 'Who are we?'

'We who have seen the light of Kastria.'

'Kastria?' a faint memory came into the Doctor's mind, of somewhere, or something, incredibly distant in space and time. 'Who has seen the light of Kastria, Sarah? Did Carter?'

Sarah nodded slowly. 'Eldrad must live.'

'Tell me more.'

'There is no more. Eldrad must live.'

The Doctor frowned. Clearly the entity that had taken over Sarah's mind had given her no more

61

information than was necessary to establish its control. Well, he could soon put a stop to that at any rate. 'Sarah! No longer need you obey the will of Eldrad. Cast him from your mind. You are free of him.'

'I am free of him,' repeated Sarah obediently.

The Doctor touched her temple once again. Sarah opened her eyes, feeling as if some mental burden had been suddenly lifted. She blinked at the Doctor. 'What now?'

'Let's go back to the control room and see how young Driscoll's getting on.'

Professor Watson was looking at the control room monitor, watching Driscoll as he hunted round the fission room. 'Found anything, Driscoll?'

'Nothing so far, sir. I'll go on looking.'

The fission control room was a small, relatively bare chamber, and there weren't many places to search. Eventually Driscoll looked up. 'There's nothing here, sir.'

'Very well, Driscoll. Come on out of there.' Watson turned away from the screen.

Driscoll slipped off the heavy protected gauntlet. The ring on his middle finger shone with a fierce blue glow. A voice in Driscoll's head said, 'Eldrad must live.'

He slipped the gauntlet back on and left the fission room.

As they walked into the main control room, the Doctor said conversationally, 'Sarah, who's Eldrad?'

Sarah looked blankly at him. 'Who's who?'

The Doctor smiled.

Professor Watson bustled across to them. 'Ah, there you are, Doctor! No joy from Driscoll, I'm afraid.'

'What do you mean, no joy?'

'He hasn't been able to find anything.'

'But the ring must be in the reactor room. He must have found it.'

'Then why would he say he hadn't?'

'Because the ring affects the will of those in contact with it. Remember Carter? He tried to kill me!'

'So you think Driscoll ...'

The Doctor nodded grimly.

In the decontamination area, an off-duty guard was giving himself a routine check with the geiger counter. As he hung the instrument back in place, he heard a mysterious thumping. Puzzled, he followed the sound to its source, the massive safe in the corner of the room.

The guard stared at the safe. The steady 'thump, thump, thump' was coming from *inside*—as though something was hurling itself determinedly against the safe door.

The guard hurried to the wall communication unit and flicked a switch. 'Security to Control ...'

Professor Watson beckoned the Doctor as the guard's voice crackled from the speaker. 'I've got something weird down here, Director. A kind of banging and thumping—from *inside* the decontamination safe.'

Watson looked up at the Doctor. 'Driscoll must have put the hand in there.'

'So what?' asked Sarah. As far as she was concerned, the inside of a nice strong safe was the best place for it.

'But it's where we keep test samples, that sort of thing. Radioactive material.'

'We'll have to shift it,' said the Doctor decisively. 'It'll be gaining strength from the radioactivity.'

'Perfectly safe in there for the moment, though,' said Watson. 'That safe can't be opened from the inside.'

'I hope you're right!'

The worried voice of the guard came from the speaker. 'What shall I *do*, sir?'

'Tell him I'm on my way,' shouted the Doctor and ran from the room.

'Hullo, Security? This is the Director. Someone's coming down. There shouldn't be any danger, but stay there and keep an eye on it, will you?'

'Right, sir, will do.'

The guard was still standing in front of the safe when Driscoll arrived in the area. Driscoll stood beside him staring fixedly at the safe, listening to the muffled thumps as if they were some kind of coded message.

The guard leaned forward and tried the safe door to make sure it was secure. 'Hear that, Mr Driscoll? What do you reckon?'

'Eldrad must live,' said Driscoll, and clubbed him savagely on the back of the neck. The guard fell, and Driscoll produced a set of keys and began opening the safe. He swung the heavy door open and groped inside.

The hand sprang forward and grasped him by the wrist.

The Doctor came into the decontamination area just in time to see a radiation-suited figure moving away.

'Hey, you,' yelled the Doctor.

The figure ignored him, and hurried off.

The Doctor rounded a bank of controls and saw the open safe with the body of the guard sprawled beside it. He ran back to the door but the figure was gone.

The Doctor moved quickly to the communication unit. 'Professor Watson, listen! Driscoll's taken the hand. Get every available security guard out after him. He must be stopped. And send someone down here, he's knocked out a guard.'

Driscoll was running between the reactor buildings when the squad of guards appeared. The leader yelled, 'Halt, or we fire!'

Driscoll ran on. The guards raised their rifles. Despite their threat, they were reluctant to shoot at a familiar colleague. The hesitation was fatal. Driscoll whirled round and raised his hand. There was something glowing on it ... There was a fierce blue flash and a bolt of energy smashed the guards to the ground.

Driscoll ran on into the reactor hall.

The Doctor arrived in time to see him disappear inside the building. 'Driscoll!' he yelled. 'Listen to me, Driscoll! Stop!' As he followed Driscoll into the huge hangar-like building, Driscoll turned and raised his hand ... The Doctor flung himself forward in a quick head-over-heels, rolling into cover. The blue flash passed harmlessly over his head, striking a shower of sparks from a metal pillar. By the time the Doctor picked himself up, Driscoll had gone.

Watson and Sarah came running towards him. 'Doctor, are you all right?' gasped Sarah.

'Yes! Come on!'

He set off at a run, the others following. 'Where's he heading for?' panted Watson.

'The fission room in number four reactor, where else?'

'But it's all shut down!'

'Doesn't make any difference. That hand could trigger off a nuclear explosion all by itself!'

The Doctor dashed off, leaving Sarah and Watson behind.

Driscoll was in the fission control room by now, sliding back the bolts on the door that led to the atomic pile. The last bolt came free, and he began turning the dial on the combination lock.

On the floor beside him, the hand clenched and unclenched convulsively in a fever of excitement ...

The Doctor paused at the foot of the steel steps leading up to the fission room. 'You two get back to the control room, I'm going inside.' He began climbing the steps.

Professor Watson turned and went back the way they had come. Sarah hesitated—then began climbing the steps after the Doctor.

Watson hurried to the communications console. 'Attention, this is the Director. There is another emergency. All personnel will evacuate the main area immediately. I repeat, evacuate the area. This is not an exercise!'

The Doctor shot into the fission control room just as Driscoll swung the combination dial for the last time. He saw Driscoll snatch up the hand and begin pulling open the door.

The Doctor heard footsteps behind him and turned. It was Sarah ...

The brief distraction was all Driscoll needed. He swung open the heavy lead-shielded door and the fierce roaring glow of the atomic pile illuminated the control room. Clutching the hand, Driscoll stepped into the blazing atomic furnace.

'Down!' yelled the Doctor. He threw himself behind the control console, dragging Sarah down with him. A shattering roar was coming from the pile, and a blinding light blazed from the open door ...

Alone in the control room, Professor Watson studied the instruments in unbelieving horror. Reactor four was going critical at hideous, unbelievable speed. The power surge was so great that it was actually feeding back into the control room. Instrument panels began to smoke, and one near Watson exploded completely, hurling him to the ground in a shower of debris. He lay half stunned, listening to the growing rumble of noise, waiting for the final, inevitable explosion ...

8

Counterstrike

Nothing happened.

Watson picked himself up and looked round the control room. The dials on the instrument panels were falling steadily back to zero. The colossal burst of energy released by the exploding reactor had simply disappeared ...

Cautiously the Doctor raised his head. The roar from the pile was dying away, the fiery glow of the atomic pile slowly fading. There was no sign of Driscoll.

Beside him Sarah asked shakily, 'Are we dead?'

'No ... though we ought to be ...'

'You're sure? What happened, Doctor?'

The Doctor jumped to his feet, ran across the fission room and slammed the shielded door with a clang. 'Nothing happened. You might say a kind of unexplosion has taken place.'

'An unexplosion?'

The Doctor helped Sarah to her feet as Professor Watson arrived. 'Doctor, Miss Smith, you must get out of here at once. If there's been a radiation leakage ...'

'Come in, Professor Watson. It's all right, there's no radiation at all.' The Doctor pointed to a wall gauge.

Watson studied it uncomprehendingly. The dial was at zero. 'Where's Driscoll?'

The Doctor nodded towards the pile. 'In there—with the hand.'

'You said that hand would cause a nuclear explosion ...'

'It did,' said the Doctor simply. 'The energy has been—absorbed.'

'There was a sort of unexplosion,' said Sarah helpfully.

'An unexplosion?'

The Doctor explained, 'Fission took place, Professor, but instead of the nuclear blast exploding outwards, it went inwards—luckily for us.'

'What about Driscoll?'

'I should think his body was totally destroyed.'

Watson rubbed a hand over his face, struggling to understand what had happened.

'The hand feeds on radiation, you see,' said the Doctor. 'Now it has absorbed the full potential of the reactor core into itself.'

'So it's still alive in there?'

'Oh yes,' said the Doctor calmly. 'Alive and regenerating.'

'I'm afraid all this is beyond me, Doctor. What does the thing want? What's its purpose?'

'Survival! To live, to grow ... Instead of energy being created from matter, matter is being created from energy. Eldrad is rebuilding himself. The probability is he'll strike again.'

'Do you think he'll go for one of the other reactors?'

A deep, roaring sound came from inside the pile

70

room. It was alive and angry, and it wasn't human. The Doctor went over to the door and began sliding the metal bolts into place. 'Who knows what he'll do? I think we may as well put these bolts back though ...'

'That won't stop him,' said Sarah gloomily.

'Maybe not—but I always like to be tidy.'

Professor Watson came to a decision. 'Whatever that thing is, it's dangerous and it's hostile. I think it's time to fight fire with fire—or rather atomics with atomics.'

'What are you going to do?'

'Call in the armed forces and wipe it out before it does any further harm.'

The Doctor shoved the last bolt into place and spun the dial on the combination lock. Another angry roar came from behind the heavy metal door. 'Somehow I don't think the Professor's little idea is going to work,' said the Doctor. 'Primitive atomic missiles against a creature like that.'

There was another angry roar, and Sarah shuddered. 'I think it wants to come out.'

'Of course it does, Sarah. It's still hungry!'

Professor Watson was talking into the red phone, his special emergency 'hot line' to Whitehall. 'This is the Director of the Experimental Section. We've got a Red One Alert.' This was the special code name for an enemy attack on the nuclear reactors. 'Yes, that's right, I said Red One Alert. I want a priority to the Ministry of Defence ... One of our reactors has been taken over by an enemy saboteur ...'

71

The Doctor stood staring thoughtfully at the metal door. Alarming sounds of monstrous rage were coming from behind it.

Sarah tugged at his sleeve. 'Come on, Doctor, let's get out of here.'

'Wait a minute, Sarah. Perhaps we should stay, try to communicate with Eldrad when he emerges.'

'What with? Hand signals?' Sarah didn't share the Doctor's faith that any intelligent alien life would respond to his attempts at friendly communication.

Watson reappeared in the doorway. 'Come on, you two, we've got about ten minutes. Air Command are going to take out this entire reactor with a limited air strike.'

The Doctor frowned. 'Take it out? Surely you don't mean . . .'

'Level it to the ground. Once I'd explained we were under attack, they were keen to help.'

'No doubt,' said the Doctor acidly. 'But might I suggest . . .'

'It's a fairly isolated area, you see. They can use their new stand-off missile with limited fall out. Now, come on, I'll be waiting for you in the car park.'

'A typical human reaction,' said the Doctor angrily. 'Any threat of the unknown, and you respond with mindless violence.'

'Oh, be fair, Doctor. What do you expect him to do?'

'Think! Now then, what do we know about this thing . . . It's intelligent, for a start.'

'Intelligent and destructive! Doctor, it's been killing people!'

'An intelligent alien life-form, shipwrecked on this

planet millions of years ago,' said the Doctor musingly. 'It's crystalline, capable of regeneration through irradiation. It's probably afraid ...'

There was another roar of alien rage from inside the pile room and a series of massive blows shook the heavy metal door.

Sarah jumped. '*It's* afraid? *I'm* afraid. Come on, Doctor, please. That thing definitely isn't friendly. Let's get out—before *it* does. Professor Watson said ten minutes, and that was a couple of minutes ago!'

'Look!' said the Doctor softly.

A tiny dot of light had appeared in the centre of the metal door. It grew brighter, brighter ... and steadily larger at the same time.

'This is fascinating ...'

Sarah pulled him away. 'Come on, Doctor, please!'

The Doctor took a last look at the door. The spot of light was as big as a saucer by now, and it was still growing ... There was another ferocious roar.

'I think you're right, Sarah,' said the Doctor thoughtfully. 'We'd better get out of here.'

Watson was waiting for them in the car park, impatiently revving up the engine of a Jaguar saloon. They piled hurriedly inside and he roared away.

The spot of light had grown so large by now that most of the door had been melted away by its intense burning glow. In the fiery circle a shape appeared ...

The Doctor, Sarah and Professor Watson were waiting

on a windy hilltop, several miles away from the Complex and high above it. Far below they could see the now-deserted Experimental Sector. A flight of jet-planes screamed overhead, making for their target.

'Shouldn't we whitewash the car windows or something?' shouted Sarah.

The Doctor ignored her little joke. Hands in pockets, he was leaning against the car, looking broodingly down on the reactor buildings.

Professor Watson shouted. 'Get down, both of you. Hold your noses and open your mouths.'

'What for?' asked Sarah.

'To stop the blast effect from bursting your eardrums. And don't look at the explosion, the flash could blind you!'

Sarah shuddered and crouched down, her hands over her face. 'Any second now,' she murmured.

One by one the planes peeled off from the flight, zoomed low over the reactor, released the fiery streaks that were their missiles, and disappeared into the clouds. Sarah peeped from between her fingers, 'Doctor, shouldn't something have happened by now?'

'Yes ... Told you it wouldn't work, didn't I?'

'Can we get up?'

'I don't see why not.'

The Doctor rose and stretched. The Research Complex lay below them, completely unharmed.

Watson stumbled across to them.

'What happened, Doctor? Weren't the missiles fired?'

74

'Oh, yes, they were fired all right, *and* they reached their target.'

'You mean they forgot to take the pins out, or whatever you do with missiles?' asked Sarah nervously.

'The missiles exploded, but they were neutralised in some way.'

'How?' demanded Watson. 'It just isn't possible, Doctor.'

'My dear Professor, a being that can live and thrive inside a nuclear reactor is hardly likely to be deterred by a few atomic missiles. It *feeds* on atomic energies, remember?'

'The Ministry of Defence assured me that those missiles were the latest and most effective weapons——'

'To you, perhaps,' interrupted the Doctor. 'But not to Eldrad. I think it's time we tried some much older weapons.'

'*Older* weapons?'

'Speech!' exploded the Doctor. 'Diplomacy! Intelligent conversation!' He got back in the car. 'Come on, Sarah, let's go and talk to Eldrad.'

Eldrad stood looking around the pile room. 'What is this place? Where have I come to?'

The regenerated being stared at its reflection in the polished metal wall. 'Can this be the form of the creature who found me, and who now seek to destroy me? No matter. They shall fail, as the attempt at obliteration has failed. Eldrad lives!'

Watson's car drew up near the reactor buildings, and they all got out. 'You two stay here,' ordered the Doctor. 'No point in confusing things with too many introductions. Shouldn't take long, one way or the other.'

'I'll come with you,' said Sarah immediately.

'No, Sarah. Keep her with you, please, will you, Professor?' The Doctor hurried away.

'If he thinks he can just go off and leave me,' began Sarah indignantly.

She tried to follow the Doctor, but Watson barred her way. 'I really think you should do as he tells you, Miss Smith.'

'What? And change the habit of a lifetime?' Sarah dodged round him and ran after the Doctor.

The Doctor was in sight of the reactor room entrance when he heard Sarah's footsteps behind him. He turned and waited for her, raising an eyebrow.

'Who found the thing anyway?' said Sarah defiantly.

'Now Sarah ...'

'Look, I've faced nuclear annihilation and mental takeover. That could have been me instead of Driscoll and besides ...'

'You're from Earth and I'm not?' The Doctor smiled. 'All right, Sarah, but please ...'

'I know, Doctor, I'll be careful.'

They headed for the reactor.

They crossed the reactor hall and climbed the stairs, their footsteps echoing in the eerie silence. Outside the fission room the Doctor paused for a moment, looked warningly at Sarah, and then stepped cautiously inside.

The door to the pile room had been melted into nothingness, and the nuclear pile itself seemed completely dead.

Sarah came into the room and stood nervously beside the Doctor.

From inside the pile a commanding voice said, 'You, come forward!'

As Eldrad stepped out of the pile room the Doctor and Sarah looked at each other in utter astonishment ...

9

The Return of Eldrad

Eldrad was female.

Strange, thought Sarah, that she of all people should be so surprised. Why shouldn't their unknown opponent be female after all? What you might call a case of Alien's Lib ...

The being in front of them was tall, imposing, majestic. Only the face was fully human in shape, though the skin was blue. The surface of her body was composed of thousands of many-sided crystals, and more crystals rose to a kind of crest above her forehead. Her huge dark eyes seemed to flash with power as she glared haughtily at the Doctor.

'How do you do?' said the Doctor politely. 'I take it you must be Eldrad?'

The blue crystal ring was back in place on Eldrad's finger. She raised it threateningly. 'Are you responsible for this stupid attempt to destroy me?'

'Far from it. How did you prevent the missiles from exploding, by the way?'

'I absorbed their energy into myself. Indeed, they gave me the power I needed to complete my regeneration.'

'I thought it must be something like that.' He turned to Sarah. 'Didn't I tell you Watson's missiles wouldn't work?'

Eldrad was studying him thoughtfully. 'I sense that you do not come from this backward planet. What are you doing among these primitives?'

The Doctor smiled disarmingly. 'Oh, just visiting. They call me the Doctor, and this is Sarah Jane Smith. Say hello, Sarah.'

'Hello,' said Sarah shakily.

Eldrad ignored her.

'I might ask you the same question, Eldrad,' said the Doctor boldly. 'What are you doing here on Earth?'

'I am Eldrad. Creator and Ruler of Kastria.' Eldrad spoke as if this alone was sufficient answer to any possible question. Her eyes flashed with anger. 'And you have tried to destroy me!'

'You've got it all wrong, Eldrad,' said the Doctor hastily. 'We're the ones who saved you.'

Eldrad's eyes blazed with a fiery blue light as she turned her fierce stare on the Doctor. His face twisted and his body glowed, caught in the grip of some alien force. For a moment he was held, motionless, then Eldrad said slowly, 'I see that you speak the truth.' The glow in her eyes faded and the Doctor relaxed with a groan.

Even if she was convinced, it was clear that Eldrad was still far from pleased. 'Why did these humans attack me with their primitive devices?'

'You frightened them, Eldrad. They are a stubborn and violent race. It is their instinct to destroy that which they cannot understand.'

Eldrad brooded for a moment. 'They must be taught to respect their betters,' she said ominously.

In the control room, Professor Watson was watching

the scene on his monitor. He could make little of the conversation, but one thing at least was clear to him. Eldrad was hostile and dangerous. At the sound of her final threat, Watson scowled angrily. He went to a drawer, unlocked it, and produced a heavy .45 calibre automatic. The gun was standard equipment, intended as a security precaution against any terrorist takeover of the control room. Several months ago Watson had been given half an hour's training in its use on the Security shooting range in the basement. He'd thought it was all a lot of nonsense at the time, but now he was glad. There were several clips of ammunition in the drawer. Watson picked one up, loaded the automatic and hurried from the control room.

In the fission room the Doctor was saying, 'Don't underestimate these humans, Eldrad. Others have made that mistake.'

'All must obey the will of Eldrad. It is the law!'

'The law of Kastria?'

'My law! I am the Creator. Without me there would be no Kastria.'

The Doctor decided it was time for a change of subject. 'Look, I don't want to pry, but could you possibly tell us how you got here? We found your hand in a quarry, you see ...'

'I was betrayed! They tried to obliterate me. Now I shall return and revenge myself.'

'Revenge? Isn't that a little futile, after all this time?'

'Explain!'

'You have lain dormant on Earth for a very long time, Eldrad. A hundred and fifty million years!'

Eldrad's eyes blazed fiercely as she turned the full force of her mind upon the Doctor. He twisted in their fiery blue glow ...

'Leave him alone,' shouted Sarah. 'Can't you see he's telling the truth?'

Eldrad's eyes blazed brighter, as she probed deep into the Doctor's mind. 'So!' she said triumphantly. 'You are a Time Lord! I have heard of you, and of the role you play in Space and Time.'

The glow faded and the Doctor's body slumped in relief. He rubbed his aching temples. 'No need for all that,' he gasped reproachfully. 'I'd have told you if you'd asked!'

Eldrad smiled grimly. 'I have learned to trust no one.' Calmly she added, 'I need your help, Doctor.'

Sarah glared at her, amazed by the sheer arrogance of the demand. 'Our *help*? After the way you've been acting? You must be joking!'

The Doctor waved her to silence. 'And what can we do for you, Eldrad?'

'As a Time Lord you are pledged to uphold the Law of Time, are you not?'

The Doctor nodded.

'And to prevent alien aggression?'

The Doctor closed his eyes. 'To prevent alien aggression where such aggression may be deemed to threaten the proper development of the indigenous population ...' He opened his eyes. 'I think that's how it goes.'

'Then you must help me in my struggle,' said

81

Eldrad triumphantly.

Sarah couldn't bear to be quiet any longer. 'Why should he help you? You're the one who's aggressive. You're destructive ...'

To Sarah's surprise, Eldrad didn't react with anger. Instead she said sadly, 'Once I was a creator, not a destroyer. Kastria was a cold inhospitable planet, ravaged by the solar storms. *I* built the spatial barriers to keep out the winds. *I* devised this silicon-based structure for our physical form, built machines to replenish the soil and the atmosphere. *I* brought Kastria to life.'

Despite her suspicions, Sarah found herself strangely moved by the sad, beautiful voice. 'What happened?'

'An alien race made war on us, and Kastria became a battleground. The barriers were destroyed, the solar winds came again, dehydrating our planet. The invaders made puppets of the Kastrian leaders. I was sentenced to obliteration.'

'But if you did so much for your people why should they turn against you?'

'My people did not turn against me. It was their alien rulers. They tried to destroy me because I refused to serve them.' Eldrad turned to the Doctor, her voice low and appealing. 'Help me, Doctor. Help me to save Kastria once more.'

The Doctor rubbed his chin and said, 'Mmm.'

Eldrad flared into anger. 'Why do you hesitate? It is your duty to take me back through Time and Space!'

'Space perhaps, Eldrad, but not through Time. It can't be done. It would contravene the first Law of Time. Distortion of history, you see. Sorry.'

'You cannot refuse me!'

'I'm not refusing, Eldrad. I'm simply saying that if I take you back to Kastria, it must be in present time, one hundred and fifty million years after you left.'

Suddenly Eldrad stiffened and her head turned suspiciously. 'I sense a living presence. Who else is here?'

'No one, as far as I know.'

'They've all been evacuated,' said Sarah. 'We're the only ones in the building—alive, that is!'

Creeping along the corridor, Professor Watson heard voices from the fission room. With the entrance in sight, he stepped back into the nearest doorway and stood waiting for Eldrad to emerge.

'I will return you to Kastria, as you ask, Eldrad,' said the Doctor firmly. 'But only if you accept my conditions. No more humans must be harmed—and we travel through Space, and not through Time. Do you accept?'

Eldrad stared angrily at the Doctor, but he met her gaze unafraid. After a moment she dropped her eyes and said softly, 'Very well, Doctor. You give me no choice.'

Sarah looked thoughtfully at her, wondering why she had suddenly become so meek and mild.

The Doctor waved towards the door. 'My—er—transport is in the quarry where we found you. Shall we go?'

Eldrad strode majestically through the door, and

the Doctor and Sarah followed.

The moment Eldrad came into the corridor, Professor Watson stepped out of hiding. Holding the big automatic in both hands, he pumped six bullets into Eldrad's body at close range. The crash of the explosions merged into a single roar, echoing down the corridor.

Eldrad stood quite still. She did not stagger or bleed, and the bullets seemed to have no effect on her. Slowly she raised the blue crystal ring ...

'Watson, look out!' yelled the Doctor.

His voice seemed to release Watson from his paralysis of horror. He threw himself to the ground as blue fire crackled from Eldrad's ring, and a chunk of wall where he had been standing exploded in smoke and flame. Watson scrambled to his feet and ran back down the corridor. Eldrad moved inexorably in pursuit.

The Doctor shook his head. 'The fool! Won't they ever learn?' He hurried after Eldrad, Sarah close behind him.

In the control room Professor Watson was feeding another clip of bullets into the automatic with shaking fingers. He knew it was useless, but it was the only thing he could think of to do ... He turned, raising the automatic, as Eldrad appeared in the doorway. Her eyes blazed fiercely, and the gun dropped from the Professor's hand. He stood transfixed by Eldrad's gaze, his whole body glowing with blue light, his face twisted in agony. 'You shall die slowly as traitors deserve,' said Eldrad softly.

The Doctor and Sarah appeared in the doorway behind her. 'Eldrad, stop!' shouted the Doctor. 'Remember our agreement. If you kill him, I won't help you to return to Kastria.'

Eldrad didn't hear him. Her eyes were fixed gloatingly on Professor Watson, as he twisted in silent agony.

'Eldrad!' said the Doctor again. 'Does your revenge on one wretched primitive mean so much to you? Release him, or you will never return to Kastria.'

The cruel glow faded from Eldrad's eyes, faded too from around Watson's body. He slumped to the ground, like a puppet with suddenly severed strings.

Sarah ran to kneel beside him. 'He's still breathing, Doctor—but that's about all!'

Indifferently Eldrad turned away. 'Come, Doctor, let us be going.'

'Not until I'm sure he's all right.'

'I hold you to your promise, Doctor. Let us be gone from here.'

'Eldrad, you owe the power for your regeneration to this man's work. Remember that!'

'Yes, Doctor,' said Eldrad mockingly. 'I have shown my gratitude—leave him, he will recover.'

The Doctor went and knelt by Watson, raising his head. 'Professor Watson, can you hear me?'

Watson's eyes opened.

'You see?' said Eldrad impatiently. 'I am not as cruel as you think me, Doctor.'

'Are you all right, Professor?' asked the Doctor.

Watson stared dazedly at him. 'Yes ... I think so ... just stunned ...'

The Doctor stood up. 'Come, Eldrad.' He marched

from the room, and Eldrad followed.

Sarah paused a moment longer. 'I'm sorry, but I've got to go with them. Are you sure you're all right, Professor?'

Watson climbed stiffly to his feet. 'Yes, yes, Miss Smith, you go on,' he said dazedly.

Sarah hurried out and Watson picked up the automatic that lay at his feet. 'I put six bullets in that creature,' he said in an astonished voice. He tossed the gun in the drawer.

A familiar voice called, 'Professor Watson, are you there?'

'In here, Miss Jackson.'

Miss Jackson came slowly into the control room, staring in horror at the blackened instrument panels and the exploded consoles. 'What happened?'

Professor Watson sighed. 'What happened, Miss Jackson? For a start most of the laws of physics have been broken. The Atomic Energy Commission just won't believe it!'

'What was all that business with the planes?' asked Miss Jackson disapprovingly. 'Bombing the reactor indeed!'

Professor Watson clutched at his hair. 'The planes! The RAF won't believe it either!' He groaned despairingly.

'I saw the Doctor as I was coming in. He was driving your car.'

'Did you see who was with him?'

'Miss Smith was in the front passenger seat. And there was someone else in the back.'

'Thank heavens for that,' said Professor Watson

fervently. He looked round the shattered control room. 'Look at the place. This plant cost four hundred million pounds to build, and they'll probably ask me four hundred million questions at the enquiry. And if I tell them the truth, they'll put me in a padded cell!'

The red phone began to ring. Watson stared gloomily at it, but didn't move.

'Shall I say you're busy?' asked Miss Jackson.

Professor Watson shook his head. 'No, may as well get it over.' He picked up the phone. 'Hullo. Watson here.' He listened to the agitated voice at the other end and then said impatiently, 'Yes, we are all right, no, I don't know what happened. Yes, I know there'll have to be a full enquiry, and I wish you joy of it. It'll probably take you about twenty years! Now, if you don't mind, Minister, I've got work to do!'

Greatly cheered up by this exchange Professor Watson slammed down the phone and turned to his assistant. 'Now then, Miss Jackson, let's see if we can get this shambles sorted out ...'

Tom Abbott was supervising the setting of a fresh set of blasting charges when a car drove up and came to a halt just inside the quarry gates. The Doctor got out and looked round enquiringly.

'Hey, Doctor,' yelled Abbott. The Doctor looked up and waved. Abbott pointed to the TARDIS which was standing just behind the work hut. The Doctor looked and waved his understanding. Two more people got out of the car, the girl who'd been in the accident and a tall woman in some kind of fancy get-up. The Doctor opened the door of the police box with a key, and they all went inside.

Abbott grinned, thinking it must be a tight fit in there, and turned back to his work. A few minutes later he heard a wheezing groaning noise, and looked up in astonishment. But there was nothing to see.

The empty car still stood by the quarry gates, but the old blue police box had vanished ...

10

Return to Kastria

The Doctor straightened up from the TARDIS console and looked at his strange guest. 'Well, Eldrad, this is the TARDIS. What do you think of her?'

Eldrad gazed around the big control room so improbably contained inside the police box. 'I congratulate you, Doctor. The achievements of your people in temporal engineering are indeed impressive.'

The Doctor couldn't help being flattered. 'She's one of the older models of course. Still, I'm glad you like her.'

Casually Eldrad asked, 'Where are your weapons?'

The Doctor smiled and tapped his forehead. 'In here, Eldrad.'

Eldrad smiled coldly. Her eyes widened, became flat discs of blazing blue fire.

The Doctor yawned and stretched. 'I shouldn't bother, Eldrad, your weapons won't work in here. We're in a state of temporal grace, you see, multidimensional.'

'What do you mean?'

'I mean you can't hurt us, any more than we can hurt you!'

Sarah didn't entirely understand the Doctor's explanation, but she seized on the one important point. 'She can't hurt us?'

'That's right.'

'In that case, Doctor, there's something I want to ask you. Why are you helping her?'

'Well, in a sense I'm helping Earth, Sarah. After all, we can't let Eldrad go around smashing nuclear power stations. Who knows how powerful she might become, or what damage she might do? Besides, I want to see Kastria.'

'Whatever for?'

'Well, you know what they say—travel broadens the mind!'

'And a stitch in time saves nine?'

'What does that mean?'

Sarah answered with another proverb. 'Look before you leap!' It still didn't seem right that they were helping someone as ruthlessly destructive as Eldrad to return to the planet she claimed to rule. They'd probably been glad to get rid of her. Still, if it was a choice between Eldrad on Kastria and Eldrad on Earth ...

Eldrad had been listening impatiently. 'Will you stop this childish prattling? Time is passing!'

'Yes, it is, isn't it,' said the Doctor thoughtfully. He beckoned Eldrad over to the control console. 'I wonder if you'd mind punching up the galactic co-ordinates for Kastria? I'm a bit vague on its exact whereabouts.'

Eldrad's hands moved rapidly over the controls. 'There! I have used Kastrian computation, of course. What about the expansion factor for your Time Lord astrogation matrix?'

'Oh, just punch up seven, four, three, eight, zero, zero, eight, one, twelve, twelve, seven, two, seven, two, nine, eleven, eight, three, four, one, one, one, three, zero, nine, eleven, fifteen, and see what happens,' said the Doctor airily.

Eldrad's hands moved over the controls. The TARDIS gave a protesting roar and lurched ominously.

'A bit off-course, are we?' gasped Sarah.

The Doctor moved round the many-sided control console, his hands moving rapidly. 'No, I don't think so ... I'd better recheck your co-ordinates though, Eldrad, if you don't mind.'

It was clear from Eldrad's reaction that she did mind. 'Do you doubt my ability?'

The TARDIS lurched again. 'Oh, no, no, no,' said the Doctor hurriedly, his hands flickering over the controls. 'I just want to make sure we get there!'

Eldrad glared suspiciously at him. 'If you are resetting the co-ordinates for some other destination, Doctor——' She broke off in helpless fury.

'It's no good, Eldrad, for once you'll just have to trust someone, won't you?' said Sarah mockingly.

'Trust?' Eldrad gave a bitter laugh. 'I trusted *them* —and they tried to obliterate me!'

The TARDIS rocked and spun, and the Doctor worked feverishly at the controls as he fought to steady it. 'You'll achieve nothing on Kastria, Eldrad, until you overcome this paranoid obsession with treachery. You've got to trust me.'

'You leave me no choice, Doctor.'

The Doctor was still wrestling with the controls. 'If you've mis-set those co-ordinates,' he said grimly, 'symbolic resonance will occur in the tachoid time crystal. If that happens, there'll be no chance of our landing anywhere—ever!' He made a final adjustment to the controls, and stepped back, shaking his head. 'Ever, ever, ever!' he repeated with gloomy relish.

The TARDIS gave one final lurch, and then steadied. The column in the centre of the control console slowed, and then stopped moving.

There was a moment's silence. 'We appear to have landed,' said the Doctor mildly.

Eldrad said coldly, 'So! Now you will have to trust me, Doctor!'

The Doctor switched on the scanner. After a moment the screen cleared to show a bleak, barren landscape, its bare rocks scoured by a howling storm. Close by a low dome was half-buried by snow.

Sarah studied the desolate scene. 'Is that Kastria?'

Eldrad's eyes were ablaze with triumph. 'It is!' However unappealing her home planet, she seemed glad enough to have returned.

'It's—very nice,' said Sarah tactfully.

'It is a barren desolation, as you can see. The solar storms have devastated it. But I will reclaim it— Kastria shall live again!'

The Doctor studied the monitor. 'You may have left it a bit late, Eldrad. That hurricane has been blowing for a hundred and fifty million years!'

Eldrad shook her head impatiently. 'Come, Doctor, there is much to do. How is the atmosphere constituted?'

The Doctor moved to another side of the console and studied the instrument reading. 'Near enough earth normal—a bit low on oxygen.'

'And the radiation count?'

'A bit high—but still below the danger level.'

'That is all we need. Come!'

The Doctor opened the TARDIS doors and they staggered out into a howling storm.

It was only a few yards to the observation dome, but Sarah felt as if she was travelling to the north pole. The thin air was bitterly cold and the wind screamed eerily, plucking at their clothing and driving the icy snow into their faces. At last they reached the dome. Eldrad opened a small door and they staggered inside. It was almost as cold inside the dome as out, but at least they were sheltered from the wind. Gasping and shivering, Sarah looked around her.

There wasn't much to see. The observation dome was a small circular chamber, with a control console in the centre. The console seemed made of solid crystal, with a diamond-shaped screen set into the top. On the far side of the chamber was a heavy metal door with a control panel on the adjoining wall.

The Doctor forced the door closed, shutting out the howl of the never-ending storm. 'Your alien oppressors seem to have moved on, Eldrad. But I'm afraid they've left this planet as good as dead.'

Eldrad was undismayed. 'Oh no, Doctor. You are looking upon Kastria as it was, before I built the solar barriers. My fellow Kastrians may not have been able to maintain the system I devised for them without me. But there will be survivors, eking out a miserable existence in the thermal caves deep underground.'

The Doctor swept a hand across the dead control

console. 'Even if they exist, I don't see how we can reach them. Nothing functions here, there's no power.'

Eldrad moved over to a section of wall. Her hands moved over the metal and a hatch slid back, revealing a concealed control-panel. 'Did you think I would not be prepared for my return? Long before my exile I set up a secret power reserve.'

Her hands touched the controls and there was a sudden hum of power. Lights blazed in the observation dome, the temperature began to rise, and the instruments on the central console flickered into life. The control panel beside the heavy metal door suddenly lit up.

Sarah looked round in admiration. 'That's incredible, Eldrad. All systems go, after a hundred and fifty million years!'

'Where's the power coming from?' asked the Doctor.

'The energy is drawn directly from the planetary core.'

'An inexhaustible power source, then?'

'Exactly so, Doctor. My gift to Kastria, the last and greatest of my discoveries. I was captured and sentenced to obliteration before I could pass its benefits on to my people.' Eldrad moved over to the metal door and touched a hand to the control panel. 'Come, we shall descend to the thermal caves.'

The metal door slid open, revealing a lift. Eldrad stepped eagerly inside.

In the rear wall of the lift a panel slid back. Behind it was a projecting nozzle, much like the barrel of a gun.

'Eldrad, look out,' yelled the Doctor. But it was too

late. A gleaming spear flashed from the nozzle, striking Eldrad in the centre of her body.

With a scream of agony, she staggered and fell ...

11

The Caves of Kastria

The Doctor knelt beside Eldrad, supporting her shoulders.

'Treachery,' she moaned. 'I should have expected this!'

Sarah saw that the spear wasn't really a spear at all but a hollow tube, a kind of giant hypodermic. A colourless fluid was dripping from the end, and in the crystalline centre of Eldrad's body there was a dark, spreading stain.

'Eldrad!' said the Doctor urgently. 'What was in this tube?'

'An acid, Doctor, designed to neutralise the molecular bonds of the body,' gasped Eldrad painfully. 'It is one of the few weapons effective against a silicon-based life form. It is only a matter of time before I suffer disintegration ...'

'Is there an antidote?'

A grim smile twisted Eldrad's lips. 'I devised the acid, Doctor,' she said feebly. 'There is no antidote.'

'There must be something we can do!'

Eldrad struggled to raise her head. 'The regeneration chamber ... level three zero six ... but you must get me there quickly, before the crystal lattice is shattered ...' She groaned and her head fell back.

'We'd better hurry, Doctor,' said Sarah. Between

them they dragged the unconscious Eldrad into the lift. The door closed behind them.

There was another illuminated panel inside the lift. The Doctor studied it for a moment, and then stabbed rapidly at the controls. The lift began plummeting downwards at sickening speed. Eldrad lay huddled motionless on the floor, her eyes closed, her breathing shallow.

For a fleeting moment Sarah wondered why they were going to so much trouble and risk to save the life of someone they had no great reason to like or trust. Why didn't they just leave her and return to Earth? It was a kind of natural reflex, she decided. When someone was badly hurt it seemed natural to do your best for them—whoever or whatever they were ...

In a hidden chamber, deep beneath the planet, a shrouded figure sat huddled before a monitor screen. A tiny bar of light was moving steadily downwards. The tinny mechanical voice of an automatic monitoring system reported on its progress. 'Intruders penetrating level fifty and descending ... Intruders penetrating level one hundred and descending ... Intruders penetrating level one hundred and fifty and descending ...'

The shrouded figure did not move or speak.

The lift came to a sudden halt and the door slid open, revealing a dim, rocky tunnel rather like a mine gallery. The Doctor and Sarah carried Eldrad from

97

the lift, supporting her between them.

'Here we are,' said the Doctor. 'Level three zero six.'

'How can you tell?'

'I worked it out from that indicator, it's all based on roots of three.'

Sarah looked round. The tunnel stretched away in either direction, lit only by dimly glowing crystals set into the rocky walls. At intervals they could see intersection points with other tunnels, and the Doctor guessed there was a whole network of them honeycombing the interior of the planet. He wondered if they were natural or constructed. Probably a bit of both, natural caves and tunnels enlarged and adapted by the Kastrians when the bitter cold of the surface drove them below.

Come to that, where were the surviving Kastrians? The tunnels seemed utterly deserted. Their floors were strewn with rubble, and here and there sections of roof or wall had partially caved in. He hoped the way was still clear to wherever they were going.

Sarah felt Eldrad slumping against her and braced herself to take the alien's weight. 'I hope that regenerator room isn't far?'

The Doctor looked down at Eldrad, whose eyes had flickered open. 'Which way, Eldrad?'

She gestured feebly to their left. 'That way ...'

Supporting Eldrad between them, they set off down the tunnel, sand crunching beneath their feet.

In the hidden chamber the mechanical voice said,

'Intruders now on level three zero six. Scanners identify as two aliens one Kastrian. Awaiting orders to activate automatic defence procedures.'

Still the shrouded figure said nothing.

There was a long pause, and then the machine spoke again. 'Intruders now proceeding along level three zero six, towards regenerator centre. Orders to activate automatic defence procedure are still awaited.'

Silence.

There was a whirring, clicking sound as the outworn machinery of the computer arrived at its own decision.

'Defence procedure now activated ... Intruders will be destroyed.'

The Doctor and Sarah half-carried, half-dragged Eldrad along the corridor. The first section of tunnel was relatively clear, and they were able to make good progress.

As they crossed a corridor junction their passage triggered a light-beam set low in the tunnel wall. Concealed hatches slid back, nozzles projected, and suddenly the tunnel was filled with a black cloud of choking gas ...

The Doctor leapt forward clear of the cloud, pulling Eldrad with him. Sarah's foot twisted on a loose stone, and letting go of Eldrad she fell to the ground in the middle of the swirling gas-cloud.

The Doctor lowered Eldrad unceremoniously to the ground, wound his scarf around his mouth and plunged back into the cloud, pulling Sarah clear. They crouched in the shelter of a side-tunnel while the gas drifted away down the main passage.

Sarah coughed and spluttered, her eyes streaming with tears, while the Doctor patted her clumsily on the back. 'Are you all right, Sarah?'

Revived by the disturbance, Eldrad opened her eyes. 'She is unharmed. These traps are effective only against silicon creatures.'

The Doctor slapped Sarah hard on the back and said bracingly, 'Stop making such a fuss, Sarah, if you want to see South Croydon again! You heard what Eldrad said. You're a carbon-based life-form. The gas is only effective against silicon creatures!'

Coughing and wheezing, Sarah struggled to her feet. She shot the Doctor a look of bitter reproach. 'The least you could do is feel sorry for me! I nearly frightened myself to death back there!'

'Yes, yes, I know,' said the Doctor impatiently. 'Help me to get Eldrad on her feet again, we've got to hurry.'

Sarah helped him to heave Eldrad up, and they staggered on.

Soon the tunnel began to broaden out, and they found themselves walking through the street of an underground city. Broad avenues intersected the one they were travelling and doors and gates on either side gave on to the gloomy shadowed interiors of massive rooms and open squares. But still there was no one to be seen, no signs of life. Everything was dark, echoing, deserted.

They came to a major junction, with a broad ramp leading upwards through a massive stone arch. They looked at Eldrad, but she was unconscious again, her head slumped forward. It was clear that she was weakening rapidly.

The Doctor pointed to the arch. 'This way, I think.'

'How do you know?'

'Oh, let's say I've a superb sense of direction.'

'Let's say you're guessing,' said Sarah sceptically. She helped the Doctor drag Eldrad up the ramp.

They were about half-way up when there was a grinding noise ...

An avalanche of rocks poured through the archway towards them. Instantly the Doctor threw himself to one side, dragging Sarah and Eldrad off the ramp with him. The stream of moving rocks rumbled harmlessly past.

The Doctor helped Sarah to her feet. 'Near thing that,' he said cheerfully. 'We nearly had several miles of Kastria on top of us! Are you fit for another stint?'

Sarah dusted herself down. 'As fit as I'll ever be!'

They lugged Eldrad to her feet and set off down the passage to the left. Even the Doctor was beginning to tire by now. 'She's heavier than she looks, isn't she?' he puffed. 'Still, when you consider that she's virtually made of living stone ...'

Sarah looked down the deserted passage that stretched ahead of them. 'After all we've gone through, I hope there are still some Kastrians alive to welcome her back.'

'So do I,' said the Doctor thoughtfully. 'Though after all that's been happening, I'm beginning to wonder whether they will welcome her.'

'You mean we might not be too popular for bringing her back?'

'Exactly!'

The passage sloped upwards suddenly, and opened out to another underground street. There had obviously been another major rock-fall, and the way ahead was half-blocked with rubble and a scattering of enormous chunks of masonry.

'That's marvellous!' said Sarah.

The Doctor grinned encouragingly. 'Don't worry, we'll get her through somehow!'

They began struggling over the rubble, heaving Eldrad between them. 'Still no signs of life anywhere,' gasped Sarah.

'Maybe the alien invaders wiped everybody out,' said the Doctor thoughtfully. 'Or it could just be the effects of time.'

'How long do you think it's been all ruined and deserted like this?'

'Hard to say in such a dry atmosphere. Could be millions of years. The place may be an immense grave-yard by now, no one left alive at all.'

Sarah shivered. 'Let's find this regenerator place and get out of here!'

They struggled on, thick, gritty sand crunching be-neath their feet. Sarah was still thinking about what the Doctor had said. 'If everyone is dead, you'd think we'd have seen a few bodies ...'

'Maybe we have,' said the Doctor mysteriously.

'What?'

'We're probably walking on them! After all, creatures made of stone might very well disintegrate into sand ...'

'Ugh!' said Sarah. 'Come on, Doctor, do let's hurry.'

The chunks of rubble blocking their way became

larger, and more dense, and at last they reached a point where the corridor was almost completely blocked by a pile of rubble. The Doctor left Sarah with Eldrad, while he went ahead to explore.

A few minutes later he came scrambling back down the rocks. 'It's a bit rough but I think we can manage. This seems to be the worst of it, it's a lot clearer on the other side.'

They began struggling over the rock slide, dragging Eldrad between them. Half-way up Sarah paused. 'Doctor, I keep getting a feeling we're being watched.'

'Imagination. No one has been in this place for thousands of years.'

'What about those booby traps? Someone must set them. And who were they set for?'

'Presumably for the alien invaders Eldrad told us about. Maybe there was some kind of Kastrian resistance movement hiding in the caves ...'

'Eldrad said the traps were set for silicon creatures. So the aliens must have had a silicon-based life-form too?'

'Yes, so they must,' said the Doctor thoughtfully. 'You know, that's very odd, Sarah.'

'What is?'

'Silicon life-forms are extremely rare. Quite a co-incidence that there should be two in the same part of this galaxy—and that they should decide to fight each other ...'

Another rubble-strewn ramp sloped up ahead of them, with a half-ruined arch at the top. The glow-crystals had become much rarer here, and the whole area was in semi-darkness.

Slowly and painfully, held back by the dead weight of Eldrad between them, the Doctor and Sarah clawed their way up the steep slope. Sarah was in the lead, with the Doctor behind her, supporting most of Eldrad's weight. They reached the top at last, and with a last convulsive effort Sarah stumbled over the top of the rise.

The ground disappeared beneath her feet and she fell forward into nothingness ...

12

Eldrad Reborn

Dropping Eldrad, the Doctor sprang forward, grabbed Sarah's arm, and yanked her back from the edge of the chasm. She clung to him gasping for a moment, recovering from the shock.

Thoughtfully the Doctor surveyed the area before him. On the other side of the rock-slide the passage was divided, an enormous chasm stretching clear across its width. On the far side was a short tunnel, ending in yet another arch. Through it they could see a stone wall, and in the centre of the wall, a massive door, strange symbols carved deep into its surface.

The Doctor kicked a football-sized rock over the edge of the gap. It fell down into blackness. There was no sound of it hitting bottom. 'It's an abyss,' said the Doctor. 'A bottomless pit!'

'It's a long way down,' agreed Sarah. 'We don't have to get across it, do we?'

There was a stir of movement at their feet. Eldrad had revived and was crawling feebly towards the edge of the abyss.

The Doctor said, 'Eldrad, is there another way we can go?'

Eldrad pointed a wavering arm towards the massive door. 'No!' she gasped. 'That is the regeneration chamber ... There is no other way.'

The Doctor began searching the rubble around the ruined arch. 'Ah,' he said triumphantly, and began tugging a long thin metal beam from under the broken stones. It was made of some kind of alloy, and seemed surprisingly light for its length—presumably it had been part of the structure of the arch. Kneeling down, the Doctor edged the beam slowly across the chasm— it was just long enough to rest precariously on the far side of the gap.

'There you are!' he said triumphantly.

Sarah looked at the improvised bridge in horror. 'You must be joking, Doctor. I'm not going on that, it's not safe!'

'It only has to last till we get to the other side,' said the Doctor reasonably.

'I've a nasty feeling it's only going to last till we get half-way across!'

'No faith, that's your trouble,' said the Doctor reproachfully. He stooped and with an astonishing display of strength swung Eldrad across his shoulders in a fireman's lift. Adjusting his balance, he stood poised on the brink of the chasm. 'Well, are you coming?'

'No I'm not!'

'All right,' said the Doctor, and before Sarah realised what was happening he ran swiftly across the beam and stood watching her from the other side. 'Come on,' he said encouragingly. 'Perfectly all right if you don't look down.'

Sarah shook her head.

'Come on, Sarah,' coaxed the Doctor.

Sarah shook her head again.

'Oh, stay then,' said the Doctor impatiently. Still

carrying Eldrad he strode through the arch, turning aside so that he disappeared from sight.

Sarah hesitated, putting a tentative foot on the beam. It seemed horribly narrow and it swayed beneath her weight. She took her foot off again.

A muffled cry came from the other side. 'Sarah! Sarah, help!'

Sarah was across the beam and through the arch before she realised what she was doing.

The Doctor was propping Eldrad against the wall just to one side of the carved stone door. 'Ah, there you are,' he said blandly. 'What kept you?'

The silent watcher was still huddled before the monitor screen. The mechanical voice said, 'Two alien intruders and one unidentified Kastrian have reached the regeneration chamber, next to this control room. Should they enter, they will be eliminated ...'

Exasperatedly the Doctor looked up from the door. It was firmly shut and there was no sign of any lock or handle. 'It's too bad, Sarah. We've got through every obstacle so far, and now this!' He glared determinedly at the door. 'Well, I've never yet seen a door I couldn't open somehow ...'

Eldrad stumbled along the wall, and tried feebly to thrust the crystal ring into a carved slot in the door. It was obvious that ring and slot were made to fit.

'It's all right, Doctor,' said Sarah. 'Eldrad seems to have the front door key!'

The Doctor grabbed Eldrad and pulled her away from the door. She struggled feebly, but was too weak to resist him.

'What's the matter?' asked Sarah.

'Keep back, Sarah. Look after Eldrad.'

The Doctor took the ring from Eldrad's hand and stood to one side of the door. Stretching his arm across he fitted the ring into the carving. Silently the door swung open.

'Hey, you've done it!' said Sarah.

'Keep back,' repeated the Doctor. He fished in his pocket and produced a miniature cane which suddenly expanded in his hands to an extraordinary length. He reached forward with the cane. As it touched the threshold there was a crackle of power and a sudden explosion, and a shower of sparks.

Sarah jumped back. 'They're a persistent lot, aren't they?'

The Doctor grinned. 'I think that's fused the mechanism. Come on, Eldrad.' He lifted Eldrad and carried her into the room. Sarah followed.

They found themselves in a small square chamber, it's walls carved in complex rectilinear patterns. A flat slab of stone stood in the centre of the room. Suspended above it was a metal block of equivalent size. At the head of the slab was a cabinet with transparent walls and beside it one of the strange crystalline control consoles.

Somehow it seemed obvious that Eldrad should be placed on the slab. The Doctor lowered her on to its smooth surface, then stood looking worriedly down at her. She was very weak now, and it was clear that she was barely alive. Her face had a hard, glazed look about it as if she was turning back to stone, and fine cracks were appearing in the surface of her body.

'She's dying, Doctor,' whispered Sarah. 'What are you going to do?'

The Doctor was studying the control console, talking almost to himself. 'I think I understand the basic process well enough. The crystal in the ring carries Eldrad's genetic code, the master print that enables her to regenerate herself.'

Sarah looked down at Eldrad. She was lying quite motionless, and cracks were spreading rapidly all over her body, which had taken on the look of sun-baked mud. 'Do you think we're in time?'

The Doctor brooded over the control console. 'The question is—does the regenerator still work?'

Eldrad convulsed and the network of cracks widened and deepened. Sarah felt she might suddenly shatter into granules of sand. 'Hurry, Doctor, she's cracking up—literally!'

The Doctor slipped the ring from Eldrad's finger and fitted it into a slot in the control console. 'Now then,' he muttered, 'Power, power ...' He began switching on controls, trying one combination after another. 'The storage cells are very low ... just have to risk feeding the whole output through at once.'

The console suddenly began to click and vibrate, and there was a steadily rising hum of power. Pleased with his apparent success, the Doctor failed to notice when the metal block suspended above the slab shuddered and began a slow descent ... He adjusted more controls.

Suddenly Sarah saw Eldrad's face crack and shatter like broken glass. 'Look, Doctor! You'd better hurry!'

'I can't rush it, Sarah. I'm only guessing as it is. We'll just have to use maximum irradiation and hope for the best!' He threw a final switch and stepped back.

Sarah looked up—and jumped back in horror. 'Doctor, look, that block's coming down. It'll crush her! You've got to stop it!'

The block was moving faster now—there wasn't time to drag Eldrad clear. The Doctor doubted if she'd survive being moved. He bent frantically over the controls, trying to work out what had gone wrong. The hum of power was rising to a roar . . . 'It's no good, I can't stop it,' he yelled. 'Get back, Sarah!'

'But it'll kill her . . .'

Sarah made a futile effort to drag Eldrad from the block, but the Doctor pulled her away. By now the slab was only inches from Eldrad's body . . .

'Intruder identified,' said the computer voice triumphantly. 'Eldrad, genocide, anarch, sentenced to obliteration!'

'Obliteration will now proceed!'

The massive block came down . . . down . . . down . . . until it met the central block. Eldrad's body was crushed between the two surfaces with a grinding crunch . . .

Sarah turned away. 'It's horrible, Doctor. The machine was supposed to remake her, and instead it's destroyed her.'

There was a renewed hum of power and the block began to rise. As it came clear of the slab, Sarah forced herself to look. All that remained of Eldrad was her outline in blackened dust.

'We've killed her,' whispered Sarah.

The Doctor nodded sadly. 'I think we've been used, Sarah. They were determined to get her one way or another. This regeneration chamber was just another trap.'

Sarah rubbed her hands across her face. 'I'm so tired, Doctor, and so cold! What do we do now?'

'I think we leave. At least we tried ...'

The power hum suddenly renewed itself, rising to a crescendo that shook the room. The cabinet behind the block began filling with smoke, through which could be seen the outline of an enormous shape. The Doctor and Sarah ducked down behind the slab ...

The console began emitting a series of agitated blips. 'Malfunction, malfunction! Power supplies insufficient for obliteration override. Regeneration will occur. Regeneration will occur!'

The smoke cleared away, and a huge glittering figure stepped from the cabinet. It looked round the regeneration chamber and saw the heads of the Doctor and

Sarah rising slowly from behind the slab. The giant spoke in a deep booming voice, full of confidence and power. 'Doctor, Sarah! It is I, Eldrad!'

13

Eldrad's Destiny

Slowly the Doctor straightened up. 'Eldrad?'

'You do not recognise my new form?'

Sarah stared unbelievingly at the colossal figure. How could it be Eldrad? Clearly they were of the same species, with the same blue colouring, the same irregular crystalline surface to their bodies. But this creature was far larger than the old Eldrad, and considerably less human in appearance. The body was huge and powerful and the massive head rose straight from the enormous shoulders, ending in a kind of diamond-shaped point. The crystalline growth covered nearly all of the heavy brutal face.

'How do we knew you're really Eldrad?' asked the Doctor bluntly.

'Come, Doctor, as a Time Lord you must be well acquainted with the processes of regeneration. I have merely regained my true form.'

Sarah nudged the Doctor and whispered, 'Why is she suddenly a he?'

Eldrad overheard the question. 'At first I had to assume a form which would be acceptable to the primitives of your planet.'

The Doctor completed the explanation. 'And as you were the first primitive he met, he modelled himself on you.'

'Oh, thanks,' said Sarah ironically.

The Doctor nodded towards the outline on the slab. 'We thought you'd been destroyed, Eldrad.'

'My enemies are fools! I gave them that machine. I designed it, I programmed it to recognise my cell patterns. They thought they could use it to destroy me! It is incapable of harming me whatever they or you or anyone else might do. I control it, as I shall now control all Kastria—the Kastria which is my creation!'

'And what about these enemies of yours?'

'I shall brush them aside. Weak and miserable creatures! What can they do in their decrepitude against the might of Eldrad?'

The monitor flickered into sudden life and a voice said faintly, 'Eldrad!'

Eldrad whirled round, glaring at the huddled figure on the screen. 'Rokon,' he roared.

The feeble old voice was full of self-satisfied malice. 'Traitor! You think you have victory in your grasp, but I, Rokon, tell you that you have won nothing but defeat!'

The monitor went dark. Eldrad laughed scornfully. 'So, Rokon, you live still? Good! Now I shall have my final revenge. Do you hear me, Rokon?'

The screen was silent.

Eldrad strode towards the inner door. 'Then I shall come and drag you from your bolt-hole!'

'Just a minute!' said the Doctor sharply. 'Who exactly is this Rokon?'

Eldrad turned. 'The so-called King of Kastria—he who ordered my obliteration.' There was gloating triumph in the voice. 'Me, Eldrad, the architect of the barriers, the genius who first made life on the surface possible. They tried to destroy *me*—so I destroyed the solar barriers and brought their miserable world to an end!'

'It was you who destroyed the barriers?'

'Yes!' There was gloating triumph in Eldrad's voice.

'So this story you told us about aliens invading Kastria was all a lie?'

'A necessary lie, Doctor, a means to an end. I knew you would not help unless I aroused your sympathy.'

'If your story was a lie, how did you arrive on Earth?'

'My destruction of the barriers must have forced Rokon to order the detonation of the obliteration module prematurely. Part of me survived and fell to Earth.'

'Why did Rokon want to destroy you in the first place?'

'He knew I would soon take his place. I was young and strong, and he was old and weak. He was not fit to rule Kastria. He had no appetite for conquest!'

'And you have?'

'Yes! I wanted Kastrians to be masters of the galaxy. Now with me as their ruler, nothing shall stop them ... Every planet within reach of our starships shall bow before the might of Kastria.' Eldrad turned away. 'And now I have a long-awaited audience with King Rokon!' He flung open the door to the inner chamber and strode inside.

Sarah looked at the Doctor. 'We seem to have been taken for a ride.'

The Doctor crossed to the console, took Eldrad's ring from the slot and headed for the inner door. 'Come on, Sarah, we may as well see the last act.'

They paused in the doorway. Eldrad was towering over the huddled figure on the throne. 'Rokon!' he bellowed.

The figure made no response.

'You scorn me, Rokon? You scorn me, Eldrad, your successor?' Eldrad grabbed the edge of the cloak with one enormous hand spinning the figure round. The dead face of King Rokon sneered at him in malicious triumph. Then the wizened body toppled from its throne and crashed to the floor, dissolving into a heap of glittering sand.

Eldrad's foot scattered the fragments that had once been the body of a king. 'What is this, Rokon! You have robbed me of my revenge!'

'But he was alive, Doctor,' whispered Sarah. 'We saw him. He spoke to Eldrad.'

'A recording from the past, Sarah. King Rokon knew Eldrad better than we did. He realised there was always a chance that Eldrad would return ... and he prepared a reception for him ...'

Eldrad's deep voice was almost a groan. 'He robs me of my destiny!'

Sarah said wonderingly, 'Then the booby traps, the recording and all the rest—it was planned just in case Eldrad should ever come back?'

The Doctor nodded, staring down at the glittering remains of King Rokon.

Eldrad straightened up. 'Yet I am still King!' he boomed. 'Nothing can stop me now. My ambition is limitless. I shall be invincible——'

The Doctor interrupted from the doorway. 'Excuse me, your Majesty. Where are your subjects?'

'My subjects?' sneered Eldrad. He pointed to a long panel set into the wall. It was covered with line upon line of angular Kastrian hieroglyphics. 'Stored in this Race Bank is a whole new breed of Kastrians. A hundred million crystal particles waiting to be placed in the Regenerator. A hundred million Kastrians who will acknowledge me as their only ruler.' Eldrad's voice rose as he crossed to the Race Bank. 'They will restore the cities. They will replenish the exhausted lands. We will build a new Kastria, and together we will conquer the universe!'

Same old dictator's rant, thought the Doctor wearily. How often had he heard it before! But this new Eldrad was powerful and dangerous. He had to be stopped.

Eldrad touched the panel and a section of wall slid back. It revealed a long, deep alcove lined with row upon row of transparent trays.

The trays were empty.

Eldrad staggered back. 'Nothing?' he roared in a voice that rattled the rows of trays. 'Nothing? What stupidity is this?'

From behind him a feeble voice said, 'Eldrad ...'

Eldrad turned. On the wall behind Rokon's throne a flickering image had appeared—the image of the old king whose scattered body now lay at their feet.

The figure spoke. 'Greetings, Eldrad. We always knew that after the premature detonation of the module there was at least a remote possibility that one day you would return to Kastria!'

'Yes, old fool. And now I am here!'

The quavering old voice went on. 'After you destroyed the barriers, after we knew for certain that life on the surface was finished, the Kastrian race chose final oblivion. Because we feared you would one day return to wage eternal war throughout the galaxy, to dishonour the name of Kastria—we destroyed the Race Bank!'

Eldrad literally reeled beneath the shock. 'Traitor! I gave Kastria life ...'

'Now you are King, Eldrad, as was always your wish. I salute you from the grave ... Hail Eldrad, King of Nothing!'

The image faded and died.

The Doctor looked at Sarah. 'Well, Rokon seems to have thought of everything.' Idly the Doctor tossed Eldrad's ring in his hand. 'Rather a drastic solution— but effective.'

Sarah nodded. 'Good for him. I wouldn't want to live down here either—and I certainly wouldn't want Eldrad as a leader.'

Eldrad rallied his energies, swinging round to face them. 'Yet I will be King! Not of this planet—Kastria is dead and worthless now.' His arm shot out and pointed straight at an astonished Sarah. 'I shall rule Earth instead.'

Sarah gasped and cowered away as Eldrad loomed over her. 'You Earth people are backward, and primitive, but the necessary aggression is there. I shall give you my knowledge, train you for conquest. I shall rule you. I shall be your god!'

'Oh good grief,' sighed the Doctor. Eldrad seemed

to have a limitless capacity for producing one mad scheme after another.

To Eldrad at least, everything was settled. 'You will take me back to Earth, Doctor!'

'Sorry, old chap, that wasn't in the contract. Single ticket, one way only.' The Doctor tossed the ring in his hand. 'My obligation to you is finished. You're in your own world now.' He tossed the ring again, caught it and slipped it into his pocket.

'Give me that ring,' commanded Eldrad. 'It contains my genetic code. It is my key to eternal life.'

'Oh, I see,' said the Doctor amiably. 'Why didn't you say so in the first place?' His hand went into his pocket.

'No, Doctor, don't give it to him,' shouted Sarah.

The Doctor tossed something towards Eldrad and shouted, 'Run, Sarah!' Grabbing her arm he dragged her from the room.

The object the Doctor had thrown flashed past Eldrad and clattered into a corner. Eldrad snatched it up—and found he was holding a kind of wand which suddenly grew larger in his hand. With a roar of anger he tossed it aside and pounded after the Doctor.

The Doctor and Sarah ran through the regeneration chamber and down the little corridor that led to the abyss. Sarah was so terrified of Eldrad that she was prepared to run across the beam without a second thought, but the Doctor pulled her to one side, unwinding the scarf from around his neck. He passed one end to Sarah, took the other end himself and backed to one side of the beam, motioning to Sarah to do the same. They crouched down behind the rubble, the scarf stretched to its full length between them. 'Keep down,' hissed the Doctor. 'And when I say pull—pull.'

They heard Eldrad crash through the regeneration room and come pounding down the corridor towards them ...

14

Sarah's Farewell

'You will obey Eldrad or die,' roared the furious voice, and Eldrad thundered down the corridor. As he neared the edge of the chasm, the Doctor shouted, 'Pull!' The scarf rose, tautened, and caught Eldrad above the feet just as he came to the very edge of the abyss ... The huge, glittering figure pitched forward head-first, down into the black depths of the bottomless pit. They heard one last terrible cry of rage and frustration as Eldrad fell, down, down, down, down ... The sound grew fainter, more distant, and faded into silence.

The Doctor stood up, recovered his scarf and began winding it round his neck. He waved Sarah towards the bridge. 'After you!'

Sarah was still staring down into blackness. 'Are we safe now?'

The Doctor nodded. 'I'm afraid Eldrad was a criminal type,' he said solemnly. 'The gravity of the law finally caught up with him!'

'It's all very well making awful jokes, Doctor. You took quite a chance giving him his ring back.'

The Doctor fished in his pocket and held out his hand. The ring lay in its palm.

'So what did you throw?'

'My magic stick.'

'Can I have the ring as a souvenir?'

'Certainly not, far too dangerous. Besides, it belongs to Eldrad.' The Doctor tossed the ring into the abyss. 'Come on,' he said, and strode confidently across the beam. On the other side he stumbled, hopping on one foot and clutching his ankle.

Sarah ran over the bridge to join him. 'What's the matter, Doctor?'

'Nothing,' said the Doctor cheerfully. 'That's the second time you've fallen for that trick! Come on, let's get back to the TARDIS!'

Sarah stood in the TARDIS control room shivering— and hugging herself. 'I don't think I'll ever be warm again, never, ever, ever ...'

The Doctor was busy at the control console. 'We're well out of that,' he agreed. 'Goodbye, Kastria!' The centre column began its rise and fall as the TARDIS entered the Space/Time Vortex.

'Do you think Eldrad really is dead?'

The Doctor shrugged. 'Who knows? Very difficult to kill, these silicon creatures.' He was studying the instruments before him with a worried frown. 'It shouldn't be so cold in here.' He gave the console a little pat. 'Don't worry, old girl, soon have you right again. These low temperatures must have affected her thermo-couplings, Sarah.'

'I know how she feels. Kastria must be the coldest planet in the universe.'

The Doctor crossed to a wall cupboard, lugged out an enormous tool box, and carried it over to the console. 'Nonsense, I've been in much colder places.' He took off his coat, rolled up his sleeves, removed a side panel from the console and popped his head into the interior.

'Well, it's all right for you, Doctor, but I happen to be human. We're not quite so thick-skinned.'

The Doctor emerged from inside the console and began groping inside the cluttered tool-box. 'Where's that astro-rectifier ...' Snatching up a tool he disappeared under the console. Sarah heard his muffled voice. 'What was that you said?'

'Thick-skinned!' shouted Sarah.

The Doctor popped out again. 'Good, good,' he said vaguely. 'Find me the multi-fortescope, would you, Sarah?'

Sarah clenched her teeth. There were times when she found the Doctor absolutely maddening, and this was definitely one of them. She snatched up the tool and thrust it at him. 'Here!'

'Thanks.' He disappeared under the console.

'I might as well be talking to the moon sometimes,' said Sarah indignantly.

The Doctor thrust one hand behind him. 'Margin-nut, quickly.'

'What?'

The hand waved agitatedly. 'No, no, forget the margin-nut, Sarah. I'll have the ganymede-driver instead.'

She slapped it into his palm. 'There!'

'Thanks!'

Sarah stared indignantly at the soles of the Doctor's boots. 'I must be raving mad. I'm sick of being cold and wet, do you hear me, Doctor? Sick of being hypnotised left, right and centre, and being shot at, and being savaged by bug-eyed monsters, never knowing if I'm coming or going or being ...'

'Zeus plug!'

'I want to have a proper bath, Doctor, I want my hair washed, I want to feel human again!'

The Doctor reappeared and said, 'Forget the zeus plug, I'll have the sonic screwdriver!'

Sarah threw it at him. He caught it neatly and popped back out of sight. 'Boy oh boy,' she muttered, 'am I sick of that sonic screwdriver! You know what I'm going to do, Doctor? I'm going to pack my things, and as soon as we're back on Earth I'm going home!'

There was no reply from the figure beneath the console and Sarah realised that the Doctor was so absorbed in ministering to his beloved TARDIS that he hadn't even heard her.

'Well, excuse *me*!' said Sarah furiously, and stormed out.

The Doctor completed his repairs to the thermo-couplings, replaced the side-panel and straightened up. Shrugging himself back into his coat, he picked up the tool locker, put it away and turned round. 'Now then, Sarah, you were saying ...'

With mild surprise he realised Sarah wasn't even in the control room. 'I don't know why she keeps carrying on like this ... There's really nothing the matter with——'

The Doctor heard a sound, heard it not so much with his ears as with his mind, a deep chiming note that came from the TARDIS's telepathic circuits. He stood absolutely still, listening, his eyes opening wide ... 'The call ... the call to Gallifrey! After all this time ...'

Gallifrey was the Doctor's home planet and the

sound was a summons no Time Lord could ignore. The Doctor hurried over to the console. 'I can't take Sarah to Gallifrey. I must get her back home. Now, what are the galactic co-ordinates for South Croydon ...' His hands moved over the controls.

Sarah marched back into the control room. She was wearing her outdoor coat, carrying a holdall, and clutching a stuffed owl she'd acquired somewhere on her wanderings.

The Doctor looked up and nodded approvingly. 'All ready, I see. You're a good girl, Sarah.'

'It's too late to apologise, Doctor. Everything's packed, and I've just got to go!'

'That's right,' agreed the Doctor sadly. 'How did you know?'

Sarah stared at him. 'Know what?'

'I've had the call to Gallifrey. I can't take you with me, Sarah. You've got to go home.'

Sarah's anger faded as she realised that the Doctor meant what he was saying. She'd only been half-serious in her threat to leave, and was quite expecting the Doctor to talk her out of it with the promise of a trip to some fabulous planet.

'Oh, come on, Doctor. I can't miss Gallifrey. I was only joking, I didn't really mean it about leaving.' Her eyes widened. 'Look, you're not going to change again, are you?'

'No, not this time, Sarah. There must be some kind of emergency back on Gallifrey. I don't know what's going to happen.'

'You're just playing one of your jokes,' said Sarah hopefully. 'Trying to make me sorry I lost my temper.'

'No, Sarah. I've received the call to Gallifrey. As a

Time Lord I must obey. I've got to go home.'

'Alone?'

'Alone.'

The TARDIS vibrated slightly and the centre column became still. 'We've landed, Sarah,' said the Doctor gently.

'I'll give your love to Harry and the Brigadier, and I'll call Professor Watson and tell him you're all right ...'

'I said we've landed.'

'Where?'

The Doctor smiled. 'Believe it or not, South Croydon. Hillview Road, to be precise.'

'I can't believe it,' said Sarah wonderingly. 'After all this time, you've finally managed to get me home.' There was a pause, then Sarah said, 'Yes, well, I'd better be off then.'

The Doctor touched a control and the TARDIS door swung open to reveal a tree-lined suburban street.

Sarah took a deep breath and headed for the door. 'Goodbye, Doctor. Don't forget me.'

'Goodbye, Sarah. Don't you forget me either.'

Sarah disappeared through the door, and it closed behind her. The Doctor's fingers moved busily over the controls, punching up the course co-ordinates that would take him back to Gallifrey. 'Goodbye, Sarah. Till we meet again.'

The Doctor paused for a moment, and then threw the take-off lever ...

With a wheezing, groaning sound, the TARDIS disappeared from the suburban street corner where it had so briefly materialised. A small shaggy dog, ambling down the tree-lined road on some business of its own, pricked up its ears in astonishment, and barked suspiciously.

Sarah looked round the quiet street, trying to get her bearings. 'This isn't Hillview Road. It isn't even South Croydon!'

Sarah smiled. For all the Doctor's confidence, the steering of the TARDIS had stayed obstinately erratic to the last. 'He blew it,' she said softly. She patted the dog. 'Hey you, he blew it!' The dog panted amiably, wagged its tail and went on its way.

Whistling to keep up her spirits, Sarah set off to catch the bus home.

Wyndham Books are obtainable from many booksellers and newsagents. If you have any difficulty please send purchase price plus postage on the scale below to:

Wyndham Cash Sales
P.O. Box 11
Falmouth
Cornwall

While every effort is made to keep prices low, it is sometimes necessary to increase prices at short notice. Wyndham Books reserve the right to show new retail prices on covers which may differ from those advertised in the text or elsewhere.

Postage and Packing Rate

UK: 22p for the first book, plus 10p per copy for each additional book ordered to a maximum charge of 82p.
BFPO and Eire: 22p for the first book, plus 10p per copy for the next 6 books and thereafter 4p per book. **Overseas:** 30p for the first book and 10p per copy for each additional book.

These charges are subject to Post Office charge fluctuations.